I0456834

The Spirit Guide: Journey Through Life

"The Awakening Tetralogy" - A Series of Four Spiritual Books, Volume 2

Ken Luball

Published by Ken Luball, 2022.

Also by Ken Luball

A Mystical Trilogy: 'Our Search for Meaning'
'Our Search for Meaning: Book 1'
'Our Search for Meaning - Book 2'
'Our Search for Meaning – Book 3'

A Spiritual Duology: Spiritual Reflections
Spiritual Reflections 1
Spiritual Reflections 2

"The Awakening Tetralogy" - A Series of Four Spiritual Books
Today I Am Going to Die: Choices in Life
The Spirit Guide: Journey Through Life
Tranquility: A Village of Hope
The Illusion of Happiness: Choosing Love Over Fear

Watch for more at kenluball.com.

Prologue: The Three Stages of Enlightenment

The First Stage of Enlightenment – Being Asleep

The first stage of enlightenment begins when we are born, as we are socialized and taught to accept the self-centered beliefs of the world. With our birth, our identity is often already pre-determined. The color of our skin, country we are born into, religion, and many other man-made comparisons often dictate our future in the world.

We believe these comparisons are true by observing others, reading about them in books and newspapers, and by watching TV and movies. Most people believe and internalize these differences, further proving to themselves they are better, more important than another.

Those who accept and believe what they were taught is true, despite their success in life, remain asleep, destined to live a life of mediocrity, believing their happiness and meaning will come from the world. It will not.

The Second Stage of Enlightenment – Awakening

Those who awaken begin to question if everything we learned and accepted to be true in life, as we were growing up, was true. A feeling begins to flourish within, no longer able to be ignored, questioning the validity of everything we once believed. Though we may be leading a successful life, be wealthy, famous, or any other comparison we learned determines what success is, it no longer quells the uneasy feelings we experience coming from deep within us.

The anguish we feel emanates from our spirit, present within every life. Some may call the spirit, god, soul, essence or assign it another name. It does not matter. It represents our guide through life giving our life meaning.

We awaken when we first sense something is wrong, begin to question if what we learned and accepted was true may not have been, beginning us on a journey we have no choice but to pursue. A journey toward enlightenment.

The Third Stage of Enlightenment – Enlightenment

Enlightenment happens when we finally accept everything we learned and believed to be true was not. Despite our appearance, wealth, accomplishments, material possessions, or any other comparison differentiating us from each other, we now realize we are not, and never have been, better or more important than anyone else.

We sense our spirit within, now fully embracing its messages by selflessly sharing its inherent wisdom and unconditional love with others, helping them awaken to their spirit's true purpose in life as well.

Though what we learned when we were young will remain with us, its influence on our life is now minimal. Instead of competing, we now wish to cooperate. Instead of living in fear, we now seek to live our life with love. And instead of desiring only what is best for ourselves, we now wish to selflessly help others, to ease their journey through life.

With this change and acceptance of the spirit's message, we move closer to enlightenment and understanding the true purpose for our life's journey.

Chapter 1
My Purpose in Life

I am going to tell you a story unlike any you have heard before. This story is going to be told by a spirit guide, who, during this journey through life, exists within a little girl named Amara, which means eternal in the ancient Sanskrit language of India. This story will follow her life, from the moment she is conceived within her mother, to her death many years later. The story will be told by me, her spirit guide; my name is Bodhi.

I am certain you are curious to know a little more about me, so before I begin my story, I will tell you a little about myself. My name is Bodhi, which in Sanskrit means awakening or enlightenment. I have been a spirit guide for as long as there has been life; spirit guides are eternal. My purpose in life is to help a living being along its journey through life by sharing my knowledge with them. I first join a new life at conception and remain within them until their death. During this genesis I am here to help Amara. My purpose is to share the knowledge of life with her, so that she may find meaning, understanding and unconditional love in her life. A spirit guide is an energy force existing within the center of a new life; in Amara, as in most life, I will exist within her heart. Within my energy force, there is vast knowledge of the history of the universe. All wisdom, in perpetuity, exists within me, as it does within every spirit guide. The reason for my existence is to help Amara understand the purpose of her life. I am here so she may learn from me and share this with others; by sharing my essence and love with others selflessly, her life will be complete. She will be born with all the knowledge she will need to live a happy, meaningful life; she will be born enlightened. This is the reason every spirit guide exists, and we will only be successful if we are able to accomplish this in order to give meaning to the life we are there to help.

Amara will actually be writing this book shortly before her death, which will happen many years after she is born. Until then, she often was unable to hear my thoughts clearly. Every life has its own spirit guide, so you can imagine there are many of us that exist. Since a spirit guide has never written a book before, I think it is important to let you know why I am taking this extraordinary step. I understand how difficult it must be to believe what I am telling you; however, I would never have revealed myself and written this book, with Amara's help, if it wasn't absolutely necessary.

I am here to warn you. Unless change comes quickly, all life on this planet is destined to end. The avarice, represented by the extreme greed for wealth and material gain by many, has led to war, hatred, fear, prejudice, starvation, homelessness, climate change, needless death and so much more; all this threatens the continuation of life. The many threats ensuring a rapid end to life are just one reason this book is being written. It is also being written to let you know how this catastrophe may be avoided. The world is at the edge of a precipice. Though time is quickly running out, it is not too late to change the impeding outcome. To do this, however, it is very important to closely follow and heed the advice I am about to give you. This change must begin immediately; I cannot stress enough the urgency for this to happen. I assure you I would have never taken such drastic measures in writing this book if it were not. It is my hope my words are heeded. For if they are not, all life on this planet will simply become a relic of time, a brief memory in the history of the vast universe.

There is no religion associated with a spirit guide; rather, it is simply a guide here to help each life embrace their full potential during their lifetime. While religion tends to divide people, spirit guides are here to unite them. There have been wars, hatred, fear, feelings of superiority and prejudice associated with religion; with spirituality, there is only unconditional love, which is love that is given selflessly. Though the ideas of religion were noble when they first started, over time, they transformed into a distraction as they accepted the many false messages learned in a world of greed, rather than the message of unconditional love from the spirit guide within.

Time is relative to a spirit guide; it has little meaning. A life that may last many years, to a spirit guide, appears to pass in the blink of an eye; that may be a hard concept to understand. Though we are present to help throughout one's entire life, to us it appears we are there for mere seconds. There is no concept of time where I come from; rather, all past, present, and future events are viewed at once, appearing to occur simultaneously, all at the same point in time. In what is considered one day here on earth, I may have been a spirit guide to hundreds of different lives.

After Amara and I are born, Amara will be socialized and taught what is expected of her. For her and others, the messages I will try to whisper to her after she is born will often be muted by the many loud noises and distractions she will be exposed to throughout her life. This book, *The Spirit Guide*, is about both our lives and will reveal what the truth is and, by doing so, answer the question so many ask and long for an answer to: What is the meaning of life?

Due to what Amara has learned, and the many falsehoods she was taught as she was growing up, it would take many years before she is able to hear my voice clearly again. In fact, it wasn't until the latter part of her life she was finally able to fully understand my message and help write this book with me. By then, the noises in her life, clouding what she could hear, were finally abating, allowing my voice to be heard clearly once more. Amara had learned to meditate by then, quieting her mind from all the distraction's life presents each of us every day. She would sit quietly, close her eyes, slow her breathing, empty her mind of her daily worries, and listen to my quiet whispers from within. At first, she was unable to hear anything, as the many challenges presented to her throughout her life were overwhelming. She eventually learned though, to quell the importance she gave to them, and was finally able to hear my voice again. Only then, did Amara hear what our purpose in life was; it was to write this book, hoping it may change the future and save the many different forms of life existing on this planet before it was too late.

We are all spiritual beings on a human journey. My story will tell you what living a spiritual life is like, undeterred by the many false learned messages Amara and everyone else receive from their ego or self as they are growing up.

We are all born for a reason, a purpose we are supposed to accomplish during our life. I always knew what my purpose was. It is the same as all other spirit guides: to help Amara, or whatever life I am there to help, understand the importance of their spiritual journey through life. By writing this book, it is my hope to spread this message to as many others as I can, so that love may finally replace hate and fear as the primary influence on all.

As a spirit guide, the shallow facade of others melts away, as if it does not exist. All I see, when I look at others, is the real person hiding behind a mask,

3

which has been hidden in plain sight, from not only everyone else, but from themselves as well. A real person is what is left after the outer shell of pretense is stripped away. Everyone who is born develops this shell as they grow up, to protect and help them survive in the world. They are taught or socialized from the moment they are born to believe in certain mores of the culture they are raised in. They are also taught the difference between right and wrong, how to act and treat others, what success is and so much more. Though it is important to know many of these things, in order to fit in and survive each day, what they are taught is also the cause of most of the problems seen in the world, not only today, but throughout history. Everything from war, hunger, homelessness, climate change, depression, anxiety, greed, prejudice, and anything else you can think of adversely affecting life may be blamed on all the erroneous things learned from the moment of birth.

There are two paths in life you may follow. One path will lead to encountering all the negative things you may experience or read about. This is the self-centered learned path or the path of the self, where you embrace what you have learned as you were growing up as your truth. The other path is the spiritual path; this is the path of the spirit guide you are meant to take. Due to the many distractions and hardships in life, your chosen path through life may be altered; instead of following the spiritual path you are meant to follow, you embrace the learned path instead. In fact, often you even forget the spiritual path ever existed.

The meaning of life is simply to remember the truth behind why you are born and fulfill your destiny. You are born with all the knowledge you require to live a happy, meaningful life. The reason you are alive is simply to remember and share this and, by doing so, to understand, though what you learn in life is important to help you survive every day, it does not need to dominate your actions and every decision you make. You are born to embrace and live a life full of love freely shared with all others. By doing this, using the inherent knowledge you are born with, sharing your love selflessly and using this for good and the betterment of all life, you are fulfilling your destiny.

The name of this book is *The Spirit Guide*. I am dedicating this book, along with Amara, to the children of the world. Who they are to become and how they treat others is mostly determined in the first five years of their lives. Though they are able to change their direction and beliefs after this time, it is much harder to do. I therefore write this book for all parents and their children, so they may use this knowledge, especially during their child's formative years. If, during these years, a child is brought up embracing a positive loving outlook on life, with respect for all other life, my voice and message will be heard more clearly. If, however, a child is brought up during these years to accept a negative, fearful outlook on life, my voice and the voice of their spirit guide will often be muted and much more difficult to hear. Not only may they struggle to hear the voice of their spirit guide, but they may never hear it again during their lifetime.

This is a critical time in history for this planet; it is one that will soon decide if life will continue or if it will become a memory and cease to exist. Though spirit guides have been here since life first began, we have never overtly communicated with those we are here to help. Though I, Bodhi, am writing this book along with Amara, it is really a collaborative effort of all spirit guides contributing as one to communicate the message we must impart to you before it is too late. Spirit guides can not only communicate with the life we help guide, but with each other as well. All spirit guides, and therefore all life, are connected and able to share with each other. It does not matter what form that life has taken. Though we are many, since each life has its own guide, we are of one mind and know what all other spirit guides feel, experience, and think at all times. So, though I am writing this book, it is really a collective effort by us all.

The urgent message we are trying to tell you is the path through life you are currently following is unsustainable. Throughout their evolution, human beings have dominated life on this planet for almost two million years. In terms of a spirit guide, that is only like a grain of sand on a beach or a drop of water in the ocean. Throughout this time, we have been diligent, allowing you to pursue your destiny and make your own choices. It is not in our mandate to interfere; rather, we let life evolve naturally. It is difficult, at times, to observe the many poor choices made since the dominance of mankind began. We have observed, trying our best to impart our knowledge to change the destructive path pursued throughout time. Though there have been glimpses, by some, of the desired path we are here to guide you on, and we desire you follow, life on this planet has deteriorated so greatly we feel we must intervene now, before it is too late.

The path of the ego or self has always been the dominant way of life on this planet. It has resulted in all the wars, hatred, indiscriminate killing, starvation,

5

and needless struggles throughout history. To see the result of what following this path through life is like, you need only to observe the world, be it today or throughout history. In this world, there is selfishness and distrust that divides, rather than unites us. There is little respect for other life, regardless whether the life is human, animal, plant or any other. Though this has not changed throughout time, we find we can no longer be silent.

The dangers from war and climate change, as well as from many other destructive forces, are set to rapidly make this planet uninhabitable. The isolating view of the superiority of human beings to all other forms of life, and to each other, has further divided the planet. The result is chaos, struggle, hate, distrust, and fear, which leads to feelings of hopelessness and despair.

By writing this book, it is my hope this negative, untrusting, self-centered approach to life may begin to be altered before the destructive impulses are irreversible. My message to you is time is rapidly running out. It is possible to live a positive, trusting, selfless life by not following the false path of the self and pursuing the path you were meant to follow: the path of the spirit guide. I am going to tell you how to do this in the hope this will begin a spiritual evolution that will change the future for all life on this planet, and by doing so, allow life to continue to blossom for many billions of years to come.

The Spirit Guide

Within every life lies a spirit guide. Whether you call this guide a spirit, soul, god or anything else, it does not matter. It is an ethereal being meant to give our lives meaning by sharing its inherent wisdom and unconditional love to help guide our life's choices.

Awakening begins when we first start to sense its presence, questioning if our self-centered beliefs about life are true. Enlightenment, though, will only happen when we fully accept the messages of our spirit guide, understanding everything we once thought to be true was not.

It was all an illusion, meant to challenge our life's choices.

Chapter 2:
The Spirit is Born

T

he story I am going to tell you begins before Amara was born. It actually begins just after she was conceived and started to grow inside her mother's womb. This is where life begins; it is very dark here, but also warm, loving, and safe. It is good to know Amara will not be alone throughout her life, for inside her, she will be accompanied by me, her spirit guide, Bodhi. It is my job to help her make the right choices during her life, though, as I am to find out, after she is born, it will be a very challenging thing to do.

I will stay with Amara throughout her life. I will be called many things during her lifetime, but they are really all the same thing. Among the names I will hear are god, soul, higher-self, essence and spirit. To make things easier to understand, consider all these other names to mean the same as spirit guide.

While Amara is growing inside her mother, I will teach her about all the good things she can look forward to after she is born. I will tell her about unconditional love, given from her heart to another, freely, without expectation of anything in return. She will also learn about compassion, caring, empathy, hope, awe, and all other positive qualities and emotions she will experience after she is born. During this brief time, before her birth, she will also inherently absorb the collective knowledge of the universe from me. Everything Amara will need to know about her coming life she will already know before she is born.

If she follows the advice I give her after she is born, she will lead a very happy, meaningful life full of inner peace and love. Though this may not sound difficult to do, I assure you it will not be an easy task.

That is the meaning of life and why I am here to help Amara; it is to help her remember to selflessly share her unconditional love with everyone else, in which a spirit guide exists as well. The journey she is about to take, once she is born, is not meant to be taken alone. Rather, Amara inherently knows her life will only be meaningful and happy if everyone succeeds during their lives as well.

After she is born, Amara will be told many things about how to lead a successful life; I will do my best to warn her to question everything she is taught. If she doesn't, though she may do well in school, get a good job, make a lot of money, have a family, and own many material possessions, none of these things will bring her happiness, joy or meaning in her life. All these things will bring is an illusion of happiness. After Amara is born, she will be told and convinced these are the things she will need in order to lead a successful life. I assure you this is a fallacy; one that will cause Amara anxiety, stress, and depression through much of her life.

The definition of success the spirit guide shares is quite different from what you may learn it to be. Success in life, according to a spirit guide, will have absolutely nothing to do with your job, the amount of money you make or the many things you may own. Though you may feel happy if you have these things, this happiness is superficial and misleading. True happiness may not be found anywhere in the world. If you look for it there, you will be disappointed, and it will remain unattainable.

If having a lot of money will not make you happy or successful, then what will? Listen carefully, for I am about to tell you what will make your life truly successful. This is so important I am going to repeat it. Everything you need to know about living a successful meaningful life, you learn before you are born. You will be taught the answer to this question by your spirit guide, as you are waiting to be born. Your life will be successful if, after you are born, you simply listen to and follow the advice of the quiet whispers you hear within, from your spirit guide, and then share this selflessly with others. Imagine what the world would be like if everyone simply did this.

The world has always been dominated by the self or ego, instead of the spirit guide. Rather than discussing everything this has led to, I would like to tell you a story of what life could be like if the world was dominated by the spirit instead of the self. I am going to tell you a story about a fictional community named Utopia: a place where everyone gets along, not only with each other, but also with all life on the earth.

In Utopia, love, compassion, and cooperation are among the many shared values of the community. People respect and help each other selflessly, each contributing to the overall wellbeing of the community. There is no competition, or any negative emotions here, as is so often experienced elsewhere. It is a community where only positive emotions exist, and unconditional love, shared without expectations, is preeminent. The inhabitants of Utopia not only treat and respect each other with love, but extend this courtesy to the many animal residents and plants of the surrounding forest as well. They realize there is a spirit guide within all living things, not only within people. How could anyone believe any different; all you have to do is look into the eyes of an animal and realize they too are sentient beings.

Money has little meaning in Utopia. Wealth is equally shared, not only money, but material possessions as well. No one is considered better or superior to another; this applies not only to other people, but to the animals and plants of the forest as well. Everyone realizes they have a symbiotic relationship with all life, and, only by treating the animals, plants, and the earth with respect as well, can all their lives truly be successful.

Love, honesty, compassion, respect, and all other positive qualities make up the foundation upon which Utopia was built. Everyone in Utopia embraces the positive values of the spirit guide. These values are also taught to the children who grow up here as well. From their earliest memories, children are exposed only to the loving emotions we are all inherently born with. And so, they will grow up, unlike others elsewhere, knowing and being able to clearly hear the whispers of their spirit guide within.

Those who are not brought up in this ideal community often cannot hear the quiet voice of their spirit guide for many years, if at all. They are so wrapped up in the challenges of their life, they instead detour off the path through life they are meant to take. Because of these distractions, they will face many hardships during their lives. Unfortunately, most will never or only partially hear the whispers from their spirit guide again after they are born. If this happens, their lives will have been lived in vain. They will search, throughout their lives, for answers to life in the world around them, though will never find it there. They will look, as everyone does, for happiness, love, and meaning in their life, hoping their life will be remembered and have a positive influence on the world. I am here to tell you emphatically these things may not be found anywhere in the world. If you think you have found them there, you have fallen into the learned trap set by the self. We are brought up to believe this, though, in reality, little that is learned is real or true. Learned lessons are merely distractions to the real path to happiness, love, and meaning you are meant to pursue. It is only by hearing, listening to, and following the whispers of your spirit guide these things may truly be found. I am asking you to trust and believe me. Helping you find these things are the reason spirit guides are here; the hope you will embrace them drives me to write this book.

The village of Utopia can serve as a future version of the world. It is possible to live in such a community or world, but much needs to be done before this can be accomplished. There needs to be a spiritual evolution, one where the mission and beliefs of the spirit guides, are not only listened to, but also embraced. To reach this lofty goal, however, not only will this evolution need to start with the children, but all others must unlearn the many false things they learned and accepted as the truth during their lives as well. Only by doing this, and accepting love over hate and fear, may this evolution become a reality.

I cannot stress the urgency of my mission in writing this book: to fundamentally change the way the world is viewed and to alter the false learned direction, embraced as reality, by the world. It is imperative this change begin immediately. Real lasting change, though, will only be achieved when our children are brought up accepting the messages from their spirit guide from birth. Humanity must not wait, however, until then to begin to make the necessary changes needed. These changes must be started now. It is my hope, in writing this book, this will be the motivation for this change to begin.

Within

Within everything alive there is an essence. Whether we call this essence, spirit, soul, god, or Yahweh, Allah, Jehovah or anything else, it does not matter. It is an ethereal presence intimately connecting all life together.

Our essence gives our life meaning by sharing its wisdom and unconditional love to help guide our life choices. Awakening happens when we first sense its presence in our life.

Only we realize though, our essence is more important than the ego, our self-centered learned beliefs, allowing it to become our primary guide in life, will we truly be able to understand the genuine reason for our life's journey.

Chapter 3:
The Self is Born

T
ime goes by very quickly and nine months soon pass; Amara is ready to be born. Until now, all she has known is the safety of the warm, dark, loving home within her mother. But things are going to change very quickly. While she was waiting to be born, she understands sharing her unconditional love freely with all others is the reason for her birth. I have kept her quite busy during this time, teaching her everything she needs to know about life. Since she already knows why she is being born, anything she learns after her birth, is simply meant to confuse and distract her; especially if it differs from what she already knows to be true.

Everything will change the moment she is born. Before Amara was born, she only had me, Bodhi, to teach her; after she is born, however, another guide will be born as well. This guide is called the self or the ego and it will accompany her throughout her entire life's journey as well. The self is here to help Amara learn how to act, treat others, tell the difference between right and wrong and so many other things she will learn and be taught throughout her lifetime. It is an important guide because it will teach her how to survive in the world. The only problem with the self is, if she follows and believes all its advice, she may find herself becoming unhappy, anxious, stressed, and struggling throughout her life. As such, though important, the self is also the cause of many of the problems seen throughout the world. The result of blindly following its advice is living in a dangerous, untrusting, competitive world. Therefore, everything you learn from the self must be questioned or it will lead you to follow a false path through life. The meanings you will be told by the self that you learn after you are born, for love, success, and happiness are quite different from mine; in fact, instead of helping you find these things, they will cause you to become more confused instead. These things must be found within each of us first and then freely shared with others before they may truly be discovered.

After Amara is born, the self and I will both be a part of her, as we are with everyone. We each see life, however, in very different lights. If Amara believes what she will learn from the self, which will be taught to her by her parents, teachers, friends, tv, movies, books, the internet and more, her life may be difficult and confusing. After all, the self is only concerned for itself and what is best for Amara; it has little concern for what is best for everyone, unlike the spirit guide.

A conflict will begin within Amara when she is born, as it does within everyone; this conflict is caused by the different messages she will receive from both her guides. Not only are the messages very different from each other, I would say they are often quite contrary. For example, the self will tell Amara she should only be concerned for herself, while I will tell her to be equally concerned about everyone else and all life as well. This conflict between the two guides is like a tug of war. The stronger the self is on a particular day, the more challenging your day will be. Conversely, on the days your spirit guide is stronger, you will feel more at peace, happy, and content.

Throughout life, there are many games played every day with others and with ourselves. These games are made up by the self and are self-serving; they are meant to stoke our ego, so we feel better about ourselves. Unfortunately, they also serve to isolate us not only from others but from ourselves as well. Everything from talking about others in a negative way to thinking we are better than they are, drags us further into the surreal world the self wants us so desperately to follow. By doing these things, while we think they make us feel better, in reality, they do not. By following this path through life, instead of helping each other through the difficulties life presents us, we focus our energy on taking care of and worrying only about ourselves. Instead of helping others, we hurt them; instead of loving others, we fear and hate them.

We justify treating others like this because the self convinces us we are better than they are, and it is normal to treat others this way. Perhaps they are a different race, ethnicity, religion, sex, sexual orientation, height, or weight. We justify to ourselves we are superior to them since we possess the best traits society embraces. In reality though, none of these things matter. Nothing I listed above or anything else, makes any one life better or more important than another. By accepting this premise, we become even further divided among ourselves.

As we grow up, we are taught or socialized to believe all these things, as well as what will define a successful life. I ask you to question everything you learn in life, since almost all of it is meant to divide, rather than unite us. Unfortunately, as we get older and life becomes more complicated, the challenges we face throughout our lives will often further divert our attention from the path we are meant to follow; instead, we will be convinced to believe what we learned as we were growing up to be the truth.

The more dominant the self is during your life, the more negative traits you will exhibit. There may appear to be some positive traits associated with the self as well; these traits, however, are illusionary. What may seem like happiness and love found in the world is often fleeting, passing when the next challenge in life presents itself. True happiness and love must first be found within and they must be shared with the world. So many people Amara will meet during her life will spend their entire lives searching the world for happiness and love, but they will never find them. As they grow up, they are taught what happiness and romantic love are; they read about it in books and see what it is in movies. Though everyone strives to embrace what they learned and wants love and happiness for themselves and their children, all things that are learned are conditional and therefore, are not real. If true love and happiness, and all other positive emotions and traits, are not inherent and first found within, only the illusion of these learned emotions will exist.

The world has always been dominated by the self. Throughout history, though there were some who discovered the truth and shared their knowledge, the many struggles of the majority continued unabated. The struggle for survival, wealth, and material possessions led to greed and avarice. And with this, the success of the individual became more important than the collective. The spirit guide was relegated to a faint memory, one occasionally able to quietly communicate something was wrong. The self, however, had grown so strong its messages and values were benignly accepted by most as reality.

It is interesting how the self not only dominates our actions, but our thoughts as well. In its desire to take care of us, it constantly elevates our self-esteem, while lowering the esteem of others. We often have emotional responses to other people when they do something we don't like, while judging them at the same time, using the standards we learned as we grow up. Someone may have said or done something that would bring back a memory from the past; this memory would then trigger an emotional response. They may also dress a certain way, be of a different race, follow a certain religion, or possess any other difference we hold prejudice against, having already predetermined them as someone who is not our equal.

Events happen every day that trigger a response from the self, usually based on an earlier event from our life. Though our actions may be irrational at the time the event occurs, the self, in asserting its dominance, brings back memories from similar events in the past. If the events from the past are egregious, our emotional reaction may be severe, as we relive the event in our mind. This may cause us to act out in inappropriate ways and may be dangerous to either ourselves or to the person who slighted us.

Every situation and event that happens in our life is evaluated by the self to protect us from discomfort, pain, and embarrassment. Depending on the situation, we will often react to the event exactly as the self tells us to. If we are angry and upset when something happened to us in the past, often, the same emotions will return if a similar event takes place in the present.

Since the self is only interested in protecting us and in how we do individually, with little concern for anyone else, our reactions most likely will not be tempered. Even if we don't overtly react to the situation, our thoughts most certainly do. The only thing that may stop the response is the calming effect of the spirit guide, desperately trying to moderate our reaction. The severity of your reaction will depend on your upbringing and how controlling your self is. The stronger the self and weaker the spirit guide in your life, the more likely you emotionally react in a negative manner to the situation. Conversely, as you awaken, strengthening your spirit guide within, the more softened your response will most likely be.

Amara, as do all others, had this constant battle raging within her through much of her life. Since she was brought up in a mostly positive, loving home, her battle was not as severe as many others, though it was always present until she was an adult, when she awoke. The constant struggle between her self and me caused her to be anxious, stressed, and depressed much of her life. The cause of these symptoms was the conflicting internal messages she received, not knowing which message to listen to. This happens to every person and is the cause of many of the psychological, physical, and medical problems experienced by so many. It is truly unfortunate this is not recognized by the medical scientific profession, for it is the cause or a contributing factor in numerous illnesses. Since the existence of the self and the spirit guide are difficult to prove scientifically, it will take a leap of faith and significant spiritual growth before these problems may be adequately accepted and addressed. Though the symptoms are currently being treated for many of these illnesses, the underlying spiritual cause is not. Only by treating the cause of the problems as well, and not just the symptoms, can these illnesses be fully treated.

Almost any problem in the world can be traced to this misalignment of values and beliefs. War, murder, starvation, greed, prejudice, inequity, are just a few of these problems, though this list can go on almost indefinitely. It appears, throughout recorded history, this is and has been the accepted norm. While it has always been this way, at this critical time in history, this must no longer continue.

This planet is at a unique junction; one where the future and very existence of life will be challenged. There is no more time to be wasted; the status quo, that has always been accepted as truth, must be aggressively challenged if change is to take place. I am here to tell you the time for this change must not be put off any longer.

Living in a Competitive World

Many of the problems and challenges on our planet result from living in a competitive world. It is a world where concern is focused only on our own success and survival, on what is best for us, rather than the survival and what is best for everyone else as well.

From the moment of our birth, we are taught to embrace the self-centered path through life. There may come a time in our life though, some begin to wonder if there may be more to life than just our own success and survival.

Enlightenment results when we finally realize we were never meant to compete to succeed and survive in the world. Rather we were meant to selflessly share our success and excess with all others, so they too may survive and succeed in the world as well.

Chapter 4:
The Good Self

I

n order to truly understand the self, it is important to talk about a part of the self I call the good self. This part of the self is what most people long for throughout their lives; it is the part that teaches what love, happiness, and meaning are. We learn how to find these things by reading, watching movies, and observing others. We desire the things they have so we too may have a successful, loving meaningful life.

We see and envy others who have a good job, own a nice home, travel the world, go out to eat at fine restaurants, drive nice cars, and have a loving family and many friends. As we grow up, we learn this is how a good life will be led and is the reason we are born. We understand if we have all these things, we too will be happy and find love and meaning in our life. We accept this, without question, as reality and this is reinforced by almost everyone we know and what we see, read about, and observe in the world every day.

We know everything we learned about how to lead a successful life is true; after all, the good self has told us so. It has also told us the happiness and joy we feel when we are with friends, family, or doing fun things is real, and we must strive to do as much as we can in order to enjoy our lives fully.

The hardest thing for anyone to understand is what I am about to tell you. This goes against everything you ever learned, were told is true, or thought your life was really about. Almost everything you learn during your life, including all the things I discussed above, are erroneous, even those things that are considered good. You were convinced, by the good self, if you follow all the rules, you will have everything a good life has to offer, and find love, true happiness, and meaning in your life. After all, everything you have learned and seen in the world has only reinforced this idea.

The truth though, which so many will have difficulty accepting, is the good self has fooled you into believing this fallacy. The ideas leading to this misconception are strengthened every day, as we observe those who were lucky enough to have found success and wealth during their life, as we too desire what they have.

I am here to tell you, if you follow this false path through life, you will have lived your life in vain. The path of the good self makes you believe wealth and material things are important and will bring you true happiness. Though you may feel happy when you are able to do and have many things thanks to your wealth, this happiness is temporary, fleeting. Even those who have everything in life will still have days when they struggle; when anxiety, uncertainty, and depression churn within, causing an unease that simply will not subside. Some who have these feelings may take drugs or alcohol to try to quell their thoughts, allowing them to hide behind an artificial wall they built to protect themselves.

The vicious cycle of life continues. The good self has convinced us, if we are not happy even when we have everything, we must need to do and have more things to find the happiness we seek. Therefore, we buy more expensive things, travel the world looking for answers, take more drugs and drink more alcohol to try to mask the true feelings and confusion we feel within, as we seek to find out why we feel this way. We may look for answers in another person, seeking to make our life whole by having someone to share our life with; unfortunately, this too will often lead to disappointment as well.

The truth I am about to tell you will be hard for many to accept; it is the opposite of what you learned to be true throughout your life. This is because the good self has done such an extraordinary job convincing everyone love and happiness can only be found in the world or through being with another person. It has thoroughly convinced us, all you need to do to find these things is accept everything you learned and observed throughout your life and live your life the same way. All learned positive emotions are conditional, dictated by the good self, and therefore are misleading. Only inherent unconditional emotions, shared without expectation of self-benefit, dictated by the Spirit, are real.

The reason more people are not awakened or enlightened is because they simply cannot get past this. Though I have said this more than once, it must be repeated again. Almost everything you learn during your life is untrue and will lead you to follow a false path through life. This not only includes all the negative, divisive things we learned, but also all the positive things the good self has told you about finding love and happiness as well.

The good self disguises its message by convincing you, if you follow its advice, many positive things will happen in your life. Though you may believe this message, since you are successful, happy, and wealthy, in reality, the question that begs to be asked is: are you?

I maintain these feelings you have are artificial and there only because you convinced yourself of their validity. The truth though, is nothing that is learned, even things considered good and positive, will bring the joy and answers you seek. These answers must first be found from the spirit guide within and only, after they are understood, accepted, and shared, may you find happiness, truth, and meaning during your lifetime; only then will you awaken and become enlightened.

Our Real Emotions

The ego, our self-centered beliefs, may give us an illusion of true love and happiness; these feelings though are fleeting, often vanishing with changing circumstances in our life.

All learned emotions, both positive and negative, are superficial. Only the genuine inherent loving emotions coming from within are real. To experience what these are, open your heart, freely share without motive or benefit, your unconditional love, your spirit, with all others.

Only then may you truly know what these emotions are and live your life as it was aways meant to be experienced.

Chapter 5:
The Spirit-Self Connection

N

ow that the spirit and self have been introduced, it is important to talk about the connection between these two. To further define what they are, the spirit is an ethereal entity within everything that has life; it represents the good, compassion, and unconditional love existing within each person and within all life; following its guidance will lead to a positive loving understanding of life. As for the self, it represents not only the physical body, but also the emotional and intellectual parts of every person as well.

One way to try to make this easier to understand, is to consider the spirit to be found within the heart and the self within the mind of each person. When the spirit guide begins its journey through life, it resides within the heart, where positive loving emotions emanate from. It is here compassion, empathy, selflessness, and all other positive emotions exist. These emotions are inherent within all life; they exist even before we are born. By tapping into the emotions of your heart, while we are alive, these feelings may be truly felt and experienced. By following your heart, your spirit guide, a meaningful life full of wisdom and love will be led.

The self, however, should be considered to be a product of the mind. Its existence begins with birth and ends when you die; it consists of everything learned throughout your life. Many negative traits and emotions are associated with the self. Instead of being inherent, the emotions associated with the self are learned and only created after we are born. Tapping into and accepting the learned emotions of the mind will dominate your view and reactions in the world. By following your mind, your self, rather than your heart, a life of fear will prevent you from finding true love and meaning in your lifetime.

There is a direct symbiotic and antagonistic relationship between the spirit and the self. Not considering the spiritual part of each person in every situation and illness is as barbaric to us as the use of leeches and bloodletting was in the middle ages or the performance of an exorcism to treat certain mental illnesses. Though the treatment may work temporarily, the underlying problem could never fully be cured. The healers of today, must evolve and move beyond their preconceived scientific notions if they want to fully help those in need by treating more than just their symptoms.

We all go through life in our own unique way. Some of us are extroverts, meeting people and making friends easily. Others are introverts, preferring the quiet away from the many distractions we all come in contact with every day. Regardless of how we are and act, we all have something in common: we all have a façade we present to the world to some extent.

As a spirit guide, my view of the world is not filtered as everyone else's; when I see others, not only can I see behind the mask they wear, but also behind the wall they have built to protect themselves from being hurt by others. We all seek to be happy, have friends, family, and enjoy ourselves while we are alive. While all these things are important, there is another part to our lives I must talk to you about. It is the part we all struggle with at different times in our life; some struggle with it every day, while with others, it happens when something triggers a memory and reaction from their past. When this happens, to protect our self, we cover up our true feelings with a mask we wear over our face to hide how we really feel. The mask not only allows us to function in society, but it also hides how we really feel from others, as well as ourselves. Therefore, we smile and say everything is fine when someone asks how we are doing; in reality though, our lives are in complete turmoil. The wall I am talking about, metaphorically, is an imaginary wall we build around our heart. This wall protects us from emotional pain by surrounding our heart and preventing our true feelings from surfacing. It also, though, imprisons the spirit guide within our heart, preventing us from clearly hearing the messages of hope and love it is trying to have us hear and listen to.

In some, the mask and wall isolate them from everyone else. We are afraid of being hurt, so we only reveal a superficial profile of who we are to others. We are also afraid of letting anyone get too close, because we know if they do, we may get hurt emotionally. Perhaps this has happened to you in the past, or you have read or seen this happen to someone else. To protect this from happening to us, we create artificial barriers such as the mask and the wall. As a result, we not only keep others from getting close to us, but we often even prevent

23

ourselves and those closest to us, from knowing what our true feelings are. True understanding about life can only happen when we take off our mask and break down our wall, so our real feelings may be revealed not only to our friends, but to our family, and, especially, our self as well.

The result of the mask and the wall, which we all have to some extent, is we live an artificial, superficial life full of conflict and despair. The conflict and despair I am talking about exist within us when the muted messages from the spirit guide are overridden by the messages of the self. These feelings dominate our lives as a result of the conflicting messages we receive from our two guides.

It is important to fully understand this: by only treating the physical, intellectual, and mental aspects of our body and our mind and, ignoring the spiritual part of our being, treatment for many diseases, illnesses, or problems we experience throughout our lives will never be complete.

By comparing just two of the many positive and negative traits, hate and love, everything may become clearer and easier to understand. Hate, as all other negative traits, derives from the self. It is a learned trait, isolating us from others, and is the cause of prejudice, greed, fear, selfishness, competition, and so many other things that divide, rather than unite, us.

Unfortunately, by looking at the world, both now and throughout history, we see a world where the negative traits and emotions of life are and have always been dominant. It is world dictated by the self; a world where so many terrible things happen, we often become numb to these atrocities when we hear about them. Mass killings, millions dying of starvation and disease, millions more not having a home to live in, endless wars, and so much more happen so often, eventually, we simply accept this is how life is supposed to be.

Love, however, is how life is meant to be lived. Unlike love that is learned by watching movies or reading books, the love I am talking about is inherent and given freely without expectation of receiving anything in return; it comes from the heart and accompanies each new life. It is not until after a new life is born and exposed to the world, this message becomes obscured by the self.

If you live a life full of selfless love, other inherent positive traits will become apparent as well. Compassion, kindness, caring, respect, acceptance, selflessness, and many other positive traits will unite us and stop the division so apparent throughout the world. Unfortunately, to reach a point where love, instead of hate and fear, dominate your life, it is necessary to unlearn many things you were brought up to believe were true; doing this will be very difficult. Although it is much easier to simply accept what you learned than to change it, this is exactly what must be done. Only by doing this and questioning everything you have been taught to be true, may you begin to change and grow. The growth I am talking about is spiritual growth. It involves changing the priorities in your life by accepting the importance and preeminence of the spirit guide, rather than the self. This is a radical departure from how life has always been lived, but one that must happen to give your life true meaning and to save the future of all life on this planet.

It is fear that prevents us from reaching our full potential in life. Only by conquering fear and facing the demons that first caused it, may it be alleviated so the mask and wall may finally be pulled away and destroyed. When this happens, an enormous weight will be lifted, freeing your spirit guide. You will awaken and, when you finally understand and are able to clearly hear, listen to, and accept the messages from within, you will become enlightened as well.

With enlightenment, everything in your life will change. The world and everyone in it will look different. There will be clarity as the artificial barriers once isolating us from each other and from our spirit guide will no longer be present. Instead, the feelings and emotions you have will now be real.

Both the self and the spirit guide are necessary and present in every life. One, the self, teaches us how to survive and get along in the world. Without the self, the world would be in anarchy. The other, the spirit guide, teaches us the meaning of life. It is here to give us an opportunity to embrace its inherent wisdom and unconditional love. We each must choose which one to give priority to during our life and, by doing so, we will determine which path in life we will follow. I am sure you may think I am prejudiced when I encourage you to follow the spirit guide. Though the self is important, and will remain with you throughout your life, it must be relegated to a supporting role; a position that will help you survive in life, though, it must no longer dominate or dictate your thoughts and actions.

We all have control over our destiny; deciding which path in life to follow is our choice. If you are unhappy and realize something is missing in your life, you may change the path and direction of your life at any time. To do this though, you must surrender the dominance of the self to the spirit guide and confront the many false untruths you learned throughout your life. It will take great strength to do this, but I assure you, as soon as you do, your life will change for the better.

The world is at the edge of a precipice; climate change, nuclear war, starvation, untreatable diseases, worsening natural disasters, or something else may prematurely end all life on this planet. If more people embrace the spiritual philosophy, however, it may not be too late to step back from the ledge and, by doing so, change the direction the world is going in. I, and the other spirit guides, are here to help you in this endeavor, as we have always been.

The Two Paths of Life

There are but two paths in life we may follow; the path of the ego or that of the spirit. Though the ego, our self-centered beliefs, will always remain with us throughout our life to help us survive in the world, it need not dictate our choices as it does for most.

It is only when we allow our spirit, present within every life, to be our primary guide, we may truly begin our journey to discover our life's genuine purpose.

Chapter 6:
The Domination of the Self

W

hat would life be like if the world was dominated by the self and the whispers of the spirit guide were rarely heard? This is the world Amara grew up in and is unchanged throughout history. There are many who do not understand; they get caught up in the belief the desires of the self are all there is to life. Though they may get glimpses or a brief inkling something beyond this exists, these glimpses are often temporary, disappearing with the advent of the next challenge in life, returning them to the reality of the world they grew up in.

In a world dominated by the self, fear reigns and is the dominate emotion. Every decision and action we make is a result of being fearful. Fear leads to hate, prejudice, greed, dishonesty, isolation, self-centeredness and most other negative emotions and actions readily accepted as a natural part of life.

Fear divides us, imposing its will on our view of the world and how others should be treated. Instead of being concerned for all life, our concern becomes focused only on ourselves. This further isolates us from each other, strengthening the self as it does. It is sad when I see a life lived in fear instead of love.

Though it is difficult to change, it is possible. To challenge fear, you must confront the cause of that fear. This can only be done by challenging the doctrines you were taught to believe after you were born. Instead of suspicion, there must be trust, instead of hate, there must be love, and instead of fear, there must be courage to challenge the many untruths you were taught to accept as you were growing up.

It is difficult living in a world dominated by the self. Besides all the tragic events seen every day caused by fear and greed, there is also the constant worry about survival. Will you have a place to sleep, clothes to wear to shelter from the elements, food to eat, clean water to drink and safety from the many dangers that exist? This constant worry imprisons everyone in a world of uncertainty, where danger and distrust dominate almost every thought.

Living in such a world leads to conflict raging both in the world and within each of us. This conflict is caused by the reality of what life is like and what it can be. The struggle, caused by the domination of the self over the spirit guide, creates uncertainty within each of us, as we try to reconcile the battle taking place.

Amara, too, tried to resolve these differences. Before she was able to, she was anxious, stressed, and depressed; afterwards, however, when she finally understood what was happening, these symptoms simply vanished. Amara kept a journal she wrote in every day to try to understand what was happening and why she felt as she did; the journal helped her begin her spiritual journey. After she Awoke and began to hear my messages within, it was as if a new world opened up before her, embracing her with a calm, peaceful countenance she had never known before. When this happened, rather than continuing to live her life in fear, she began to live it with love and hope instead.

Religion has and continues to play a large role in life. Though the ideals of religions may have once been pure and spiritual, most religions simply devolved and were overtaken by the dominance of the self. As such, this book, though spiritual, is not religious. Spirituality is simply accepting the loving path of the spirit guide, without all the ceremonies, frailties, and distractions of organized religion.

In the world of the self, struggle for survival is evident every day. This struggle is not only for the basic needs every life requires, but also for finding joy, happiness, and meaning in life as well. The world is very competitive, with each person concerned only for their own or their family's survival. There is a me first mentality pervading every action in this world, with little concern given to anyone else or any other form of life. Animals are treated as inferior, often killed needlessly for food or pelts for clothes, even though synthetic alternatives are now available. People who are struggling, perhaps without shelter, water, or food to eat, are often disregarded in the apathy of a world where, instead of compassion, there is only self-preservation. There is so much senseless death, hunger, and struggle, a numbness develops over time, as many of the horrors seen every day throughout the world are simply ignored and accepted as the norm. Instead of helping each other and being outraged by this, we accept these things as the status quo and do our best to rationalize these inequities.

Prejudice, which is learned, is rampant and a cause of much of the fear, injustice, and hate seen throughout the world. We judge others by their race, ethnicity, weight, sex, religion, appearance, job, wealth, and any other distinction that can be thought of. In the world of the self, there is a constant need to prove we are better than others. We, therefore, display our superiority by acting or dressing a certain way; we may also talk down to or treat others with a lack of respect and compassion. In our need to prove our self-worth, we may abuse others as well, unconcerned about the negative effects it may have on them.

The self encourages fear, hate, and prejudice; there is no place for it in an enlightened society. These emotions further divide us and only help enforce the false path in life we are tricked into believing and following. In truth, absolutely no one is better than or superior to another. This not only applies to people, but to all other forms of life as well.

These, and many other harmful negative emotions, dominate a society that is self-oriented. The many problems seen around the world are a direct result of these things. Throughout the years, I have observed many attempts to find the spiritual part of life. Though these attempts were made in good faith, the realities of life often derailed these efforts. Though some religions rightfully preached you are your brother's keeper and to treat others with respect and as you wish to be treated yourself, these basic tenets about life were quickly forgotten, replaced instead by a self-centered egoistic approach to life. Instead of being concerned for your brother and all life, we became focused only on ourselves. And, instead of treating others and all life with the same respect as we ourselves hoped to be treated, we began to look at others with disdain, becoming numb to their feelings or hopes. In this competitive world, we understand our survival, at any cost, is more important than another's.

Living in a world, as seen through the eyes of the self, is difficult and challenging. Many physical and mental illnesses, including stress, anxiety, and depression, result from the internal conflict between the self and spirit guide ongoing within each of us. The estrangement we develop towards many we meet during our lifetime, including some who are closest to us, is because of the false messages we learned as we were growing up. We get angry because of something someone did or said and therefore, we demean their worth by talking down to them or treating them badly. We then distance ourselves from them, further isolating us from each other. Rather than embrace what we have in common, within each of us, instead we accept the isolating norms we learned as we were growing up. Though we may have friends and family, unless these connections are wholehearted, from within, the closeness felt is often artificial and transient. The cause of such apathy is a direct result of accepting this as the norm, instead of challenging it at every opportunity. In fact, almost any problem or negative thought about another can be traced to accepting the self's point of view.

In a world dominated by the self, beside illnesses, there is also the hurdle of drugs and alcohol used to dull the mind and ease the pain of everyday life. In trying to escape our problems and enjoy ourselves, we take these artificial substances. However, the drugs and alcohol only further isolate us not only from each other, but from ourselves as well.

Something interesting happens to many people about halfway through their life, usually in their early 40s; it is called a mid-life crisis. They begin to reflect and reevaluate their life, feeling something has been missing. Though they may be very successful in life, they have a feeling, from deep within, perhaps they chose the wrong path. At this point, they may be living a good life and have enough money to do anything they want, but a feeling within keeps gnawing at them; this unrelenting feeling may cause them to decide to change the entire direction of their life. All they know is they are not happy, despite being successful and doing everything right they had been taught. They, therefore, quit their job and often radically decide to do something else.

This gnawing feeling comes from the spirit guide, as the wall surrounding their heart and containing its essence, begins to crack. Though the message is not clear, its stubborn persistence will not stop. Finally, unable to contain it any longer, they feel a restlessness within and a realization their life lacks meaning. With this crisis, comes an awakening of the spirit guide within, as they begin to question and reevaluate everything they had learned and believed to be true.

Their relationships may also change dramatically at this time. As they begin to awaken, they may find it difficult to relate to their friends, family, or spouse who have not begun this new journey they are on. Those they knew before are often stuck in the petty self-absorbed world they continue to live in. This world, based on the many untruths learned and accepted as real, now appears superficial to them. What is important to others, which is everything taught by the self and which they still believe to be true, is no longer meaningful to them. The domination of the self, which had almost total control over their actions until this point in their life, begins to relinquish its iron grip, allowing them not only to question everything, but also to change their outlook on life as well.

Taking such a new direction in your life will be extremely difficult and may bring major changes to your life and relationships. Once you begin this process, though, there is no choice but to continue it. When you begin to awaken, life will unalterably be changed forever; nothing will ever be the same again.

This is what happened to Amara, as it does to so many who begin to awaken. As Amara began to change, she noticed her friends, husband, and family did not. What they still thought was important, now held little meaning or interest for her. She slowly began to become distant from them as they continued to live in the world of the self. Eventually, she and her husband divorced, as they no longer had much in common or believed in the same things. Amara also quit her job, which she had always hated, and went back to school. She became a nurse so she would be able to help people in their time of need. Her demeanor was much calmer now; she was no longer worried about many of the things in life that had stressed her out before. Even her relationship with her three children changed dramatically. Instead of talking at her children and telling them what they had to do, she now listened to them instead. And instead of continuing to exist in a harsh competitive world, Amara's heart was now full of love, as she was able to share her joy with everyone she met. Though she became more distant from those she knew before, after Amara awoke, some of those closest to her began to change as well. They saw her new, calm, peaceful countenance and began to realize themselves they too wanted to feel this way and thus began to question their views about life as well.

This is how change begins and why it is critically important to share your heart with others after you start down the road to enlightenment. Your change will affect numerous others, as they meet and get to know you; when this happens, they too may begin to question themselves and their path through life as well. Every encounter with someone your life intersects with will have an influence on both them and you. This intersection may be the result of meeting them, a friendship, brief encounter, or reading a book either you or they read or wrote. After you awaken, the number of others whose life you will affect will begin to increase exponentially, and with this, their path in life may be altered as well. The premise here is their altered path in life will also affect many others they go on to intersect with, and this pattern will continue to repeat itself ad infinitum, forevermore.

I am therefore writing this book to try to awaken as many people as I can, in the hope of starting a spiritual evolution before it is too late. This is a critical time in history. The potential for mass destruction of life has never been greater. Now, though, we must vanquish these and all other dangers. We have the ability today to grow enough food and provide shelter for warmth and safety for everyone who is alive; we also can end the threat of nuclear proliferation and the destruction of our planet by climate change. All that is missing is the will to do so. To begin, there must be a monumental shift of consciousness. That is why I, and my fellow spirit guides, can no longer sit idly by, observe, and do nothing and is why I am writing this book.

Spiritual Insanity

Psychology defines insanity as a severely disordered state of the mind. Albert Einstein defined insanity as doing the same thing over and over, expecting different results. What is the cause of spiritual insanity?

Spiritual insanity is caused by living in a self-centered world, where war, hunger, homelessness, greed, prejudice, inequity, exist, accepting the reality and helplessness these conditions cause. We therefore settle into a pattern of self-preservation, concerned only for our own survival and success in the world, rather than being concerned for any others.

We have the ability today to feed the hungry, house those without shelter, treat climate change by accepting green alternatives. What prevents us from doing this is greed of the few dictating the needs of the many. It is not too late to treat the causes of spiritual insanity, though the window for change may be rapidly closing.

Unless we aggressively tackle the underlying causes of spiritual insanity together, and rid the world of the above scourges, there may not be an inhabitable world left for our children to live in.

Chapter 7:
The First Five Years of Life

B

efore the spirit is born, before we first enter the world, we are born with a clean slate. There are no learned emotions or anything else to confuse the inherent knowledge within all life. Since the self will not become part of our life until we take our first breath, all we know is the unconditional love our Spirit guide shared with us in utero.

Everything changes though after we are born. From that moment until our death, the self's influence on each life is unmistakable. As we learn and are socialized to accept the mores of society, our light within, begins to dim.

I would like to tell you what the first five years of Amara's life were like. It is a common story, as she was learning how to survive in the world, much like you did. During these years, Amara, as all children do, believed wholeheartedly what she was told. She embraced the messages she heard from her parents, pre-school teachers, church, tv, movies, books she was read and from everything she was exposed to. She heard how she was expected to act and what to believe. It is during these early years, children's basic beliefs and values about life are formed. As this socialization is happening, the self becomes stronger, often muting the underlying messages from the spirit guide within. The messages a child receives from both the self and the spirit guide are frequently contradictory and cause conflict within the child. This conflict may last for many years, perhaps even their entire lives. The result of this conflict may manifest itself during their life in any number of psychological or medical problems, as well as societal problems. Thus, it is during these early years fear, hate, prejudice, selfishness, and so many other negative traits are formed, which may be reflected in how the child will act and view the world throughout the rest of their life.

Imagine a world where, instead of learning negative traits, children learned only positive ones. What, if during these years, a child learns about courage instead of fear, love instead of hate, acceptance instead of prejudice, and selflessness instead of selfishness?

Though my story is about Amara, it is representative of everyone who has a spirit guide. This could be any one of their stories as well.

The hardest thing I had to do was observe Amara as she was exposed to the many false messages she received every day. Though I tried to intervene, until she was truly ready to ask me for help and listen to my advice, there was little I could do. I, much like all spirit guides, am helpless when it came to stopping the daily barrage of misinformation she received. Her parents, teachers and others were molding her to neatly conform to society's mores and rules. She also learned from tv shows, movies, books and even the internet, which toddlers can actually play games and watch videos on now. Amara, as all children of this age, eagerly absorbed and believed everything she was taught.

During these years, Amara learned how to behave, treat others, tell the difference between right and wrong, good and bad, and so many other things. She also learned what life was really like. She would see people and animals die in some of the movies she watched with her parents; she also saw many of the other horrors that existed in the world as well. Though her parents told her none of this was real, at this tender young age, she learned and believed this was really how life is supposed to be.

How you treat other people is also learned during this time. Most are taught, to fit in and have others like you, they may need to compromise their beliefs and values. In our desire to be accepted, we often treat others without respect, joining other small-minded children as they pick on others who are weaker or unlike them. Though children may feel, deep inside, it is wrong to act or treat others this way, they still join in. They do this because they were taught it was alright to act like this by the self, which is only concerned with what is best for them and has little interest for anyone else.

By the time Amara was five years old, she had a great understanding of the world. Her self was mostly formed and molded her to fit in and get along with others. She had learned how to act and understood everything she had learned during these years was true. These beliefs became the foundation of her life and, though I would try hard to help her understand almost everything she learned was wrong, it would be many years until she was finally able to listen and begin to hear me again.

As Amara got older, the effect of what she learned during the earliest years of her life, became more evident. The internal battles, caused by the different messages she received from the self and me, became more apparent. This confusion led her to become anxious, stressed, and depressed. Her life was in constant turmoil, as she withdrew from others due to her lack of confidence and unhappiness. She had few real friends as well; she was afraid of being hurt if she removed her mask and revealed her true feelings to others. Everyone was fooled, however. Amara always had a smile on her face and told everyone she was doing well. In reality though, it was all an act. She had learned at a very young age what was expected of her. With the help of her mask, she was able to fool her parents and others by feigning her own happiness.

The first five years of life not only affects the rest of each person's childhood, but also has a profound effect on the rest of their adult life as well. As Amara became an adult, she still believed and accepted many of the things she learned during those earliest years as the truth. She still smiled a lot and told everyone she was happy, though nothing had really changed. Amara still felt anxious and depressed as she struggled to survive in the competitive selfish world she lived. Though she sought help to treat her emotional problems, the medications and counseling she received improved things only a little. The reason traditional treatments could not completely treat her afflictions is because they only treated part of her illness, the medical and psychological part, while ignoring the contributing underlying spiritual cause, resulting from the internal conflict between her self and spirit guide.

As Amara grew up, I was always with her. However, my voice was so muted and overpowered by the self she rarely heard my whispers. Though her anxiety and depression began when she was a child, they continued to fester and became worse when she was an adult. Soon, she was married, had three children, a house, two cars, a full-time job, and was overwhelmed by the pressures she faced every day, both at home and at work. She constantly struggled, trying to survive in a dark world where competition and selfishness dominated. During this time, Amara began to question many things in her life. She was tired of all the mundane things she experienced, as well as the constant stress and anxiety she felt every day. Slowly, she began to wonder if there was more to life than this.

It was at that point my whispers began to become louder and penetrate the wall the self had built to isolate me. Amara, once again, was beginning to be able to hear me as the first cracks in the wall appeared and she started to awaken. I told Amara the underlying cause of her stress, anxiety, and depression was secondary to her doubts about what she had learned and believed to be true growing up. The false happy front she put on at work, for her friends, and in front of her family at home took so much energy she was both physically and mentally exhausted.

As my messages became louder and her wall further cracked, Amara began to understand there was an alternative path through life available to her; one where love, compassion, and selflessness would replace the fear, indifference, doubt, and self-centeredness she felt. Though it took several more years before Amara could fully understand and accept this, I am proud to say she finally did. And with this understanding, the façade Amara had always presented to the world vanished, replaced instead by a sincere, calm, peaceful countenance. Also, the stress, anxiety, and depression, that had plagued her for most of her life, disappeared as well. Once the underlying cause of her problems were addressed, the symptoms vanished, as if they never existed. At this point in her life, her wall and mask were discarded, no longer necessary to protect her; Amara had become enlightened.

Amara's story could have been about anyone. The illnesses she suffered, that improved after she awoke, can be expanded on to include a range of other medical and psychological illnesses as well. As such, Amara's story can be your story.

The question many parents need to ask themselves is whether they want their child to grow up being concerned only about themselves and what is best for them, uncaring and lacking compassion, or whether they prefer their child to be genuine, loving, and considerate of others. Children who are taught their needs are more important and they are better than others, will often follow the former path. These children's interactions with others are mostly superficial; they are also very impressionable, as they try to fit into the crowd and make friends. They may begin to be mean to others, so their friends will like them. These children have been raised to believe in the self's view of life and this is reflected in their interactions, not only in school, but often throughout their lives as well. As such, they may change little when they are an adult.

The other way a child may be raised is to help them understand truths in opposition to the ones discussed above. During the first five years of a child's life, if they are brought up to respect all life and are exposed to the meaning of unconditional love, compassion, and the importance of every life, then their life may turn out quite differently. These children were also encouraged to share other positive emotions with others as well. They are thus brought up to have a positive view of the world, seeing light instead of darkness in all situations. The children in this group are taught, during their formative years, to embrace the view of the Spirit guide. When they start school, they are therefore more likely not to be a follower but to embrace all children, including those who are different from them. They will be the first to make friends with a disabled or minority child, as well as children who have difficulty fitting in or getting along with others. They will revel in the joy that comes from being there to help and encourage others, and they will be liked because of their compassion and kindness.

As a parent, you get to choose which of the above two scenarios you would like for your child. It is my hope you choose which path through life your child will learn wisely, for not only will it affect how they act in school, but may also affect them throughout the rest of their life as well.

As a child grows older and becomes an adult, they may begin to wonder about some of the things they were taught. They begin to question what they learned about fear, hate, and prejudice, among other things, and they wonder if they must accept this view of the world or if, perhaps, things can be improved. As they begin to question these things, they also begin to question everything in their life. It is at this time in their life, the quiet whispers of their spirit guide begin to be heard once more. For some, these whispers only begin when they are much older or not at all, though for others, they may begin much earlier in their life.

As these whispers become louder and begin to interfere with all they thought was true, confusion begins to grow. This confusion results from the contrary messages they are now receiving from within. As more of their learned beliefs are challenged, the more anxious, depressed, and stressed they become. Their mind becomes so overwhelmed with conflict, they often become debilitated. Unfortunately, after you begin to awaken, these are the first steps you must go through. Confusion swirls in your mind as you try to make sense of the differences between what you learned and what you inherently know, in your heart, to be true.

How long this uneasy feeling will last vary from person to person; however, the stronger the self becomes during the first five years of life, by what you were taught and told to be the truth, the longer and more challenging this period of unease will be. Conversely, the more the spirit guide is encouraged to develop during these early impressionable years, the easier it will be to confront these feelings and the shorter the duration they will last. As an adult, this conflict must be addressed and resolved. However, it is a direct result of what happens during the first five years of one's life. The irony of life is we may spend our entire lives undoing the damage done during those early formative years.

It is very important that you reread the above statement; I am talking about how severe the internal conflicts, along with the accompanying stress, anxiety, and depression, you may experience throughout the rest of your life, will be. For children who are brought up believing and accepting the individualistic, self-centered egoistic approach to life, not only will their conflicts last longer, often well into their adult life, but their symptoms will be more severe as well. Conversely, for children in which a respectful, loving, positive approach to life is encouraged, there will be much less internal conflict and they will be happier and more well-adjusted.

The answers, not only to Amara's illnesses and problems, but also to many other problems seen around the world, are so incredibly simple. As a spirit guide, I can clearly see what is wrong as well as how the world must change. When a child is born, they are innocent, not yet exposed to the harsh realities of the world. Their light is bright, undimmed by what they will soon witness. After they are born, however, with each passing day, their light begins to dim, often a little more each day. How much it will dim during the critical first five years of their life is a result of everything they have been taught and learned during this time. The dimmer their light by the age of five, the harder that child's journey through life will be.

It is my hope, with this knowledge and a fundamental change in how our children are brought up, their light will remain brighter and their journey through life will therefore be easier and more meaningful.

Raising Our Children with Love

What is learned during the first five years of a child's life, may affect their entire life. The many struggles we have throughout our lives often result from the self-centered beliefs we developed and accepted during these early, impressionable years, when we learn about our relationship with the world.

We then often spend the rest of our life undoing the harm done during these vulnerable years. Let us therefore strive to raise our children embracing love rather of fear, allowing their life to be happier and more meaningful.

Chapter 8:
Living a Positive Life

T

here are two ways life may be approached: it may be viewed in either a negative or a positive way. How the world is seen determines not only how you relate to other people, but also relates to your overall happiness and well-being. The choice of whether the world will be seen in a negative or positive light is often determined during the first five years of life as well. As such, parents have a lot of influence on their children during these early formative years and can often help shape their views and opinions about the world for many years to come.

The majority of the world views life as a struggle, in which each person has to worry and be concerned only about themselves or immediate family, rather than anyone else. Children who are brought up like this, who put their own needs before everyone else's, often develop a negative view of the world and believe it is dangerous. Though many will say it is important to instill these beliefs in a child during their formative years, I assure you it is not; in fact, the opposite is actually true. Though a child must be made aware of the physical dangers they will face in the world during this time, such as stepping into a busy highway, they must also learn about compassion, caring, respect, empathy, thoughtfulness, sharing, and all the other positive traits and qualities as well.

When life is viewed through a negative lens, the world will appear dark, and the choices made will often be reflected through a negative prism as well. Those who go through life this way will generally experience stress, loneliness, unhappiness, depression, and anxiety and will often judge others in an untrusting way. They view the world as competitive and, rather than hoping for everyone's success, their focus remains only on their success and on themselves.

What I am about to tell you may sound quite radical: be concerned for others as much as you are for yourself. If we look at the world today, a world overwhelmingly dominated by the self and its negative view of life, this idea may not seem so outlandish. After all, many of the emotions we experience, be it fear, anger, hate, apathy, or prejudice, may be traced to this view of life. There are also many illnesses, such as depression and anxiety, as well as numerous other psychiatric, psychosomatic, and medical problems that may be caused by a negative outlook on life as well.

There are many examples of negative people in the world and comparatively, relatively few of those who are positive. In a negative world, the hungry, poor, and homeless are often ignored, money is considered more important than people, and concern for everyone is replaced by concern only for ourselves. Living in this world, the self dominates our choices in life. As such, a negative person will often struggle to find happiness, love, and meaning throughout their life.

Life does not have to be this way though. If, during their earliest years, children were taught to embrace the positive aspects and emotions of life, then their life may be quite different. It is possible to bring up a child with a positive outlook on life and thus open their world to light, rather than darkness. Raising a child in a positive way does not mean they will not learn how to survive in the world. It only means their outlook on how they view others and themselves will be different. The self will always be a part of their life. It will teach children how to act, treat others and get along in the world. But, instead of the self dominating their lives, it will be relegated to a secondary supporting role. It will still be there to help and teach children, but its negative influences may be mitigated simply by emphasizing the many positive traits and qualities life offers. Such a child will have the best of both worlds; learning to survive in the world from the self, while embracing unconditional love, compassion, empathy, respect, and all other positive qualities and traits from the spirit guide. Bringing up a child this way will result in a very well-adjusted person that accepts the positive aspects of life, all the while understanding and learning the mores of the culture in which they are raised.

If a child is brought up like this, instead of hate, they will see others with love, instead of judgment, they will learn acceptance, and instead of being concerned only for themselves, they will feel compassion and empathy for everyone. This is the world we are meant to live in; it is a world dominated by the spirit guide, rather than the self. I am here to tell you living in such a world is possible.

Take a moment and look closely at the world; concentrate on all the difficulties, tragedies, wars, senseless deaths, and struggles seen every day in every part of the world. As a society, we have reached a point where we have become so insensitive to the suffering of others, we barely react to these hardships anymore. Is this the world we want to live or raise our children in?

If your answer is yes, then nothing needs to be done. The world will simply continue as it has and is now, and within a relatively short period of time, climate change, overpopulation, war, starvation, or disease will simply end all life on earth. If, however, the answer to the above question is no, then I would like to tell you what living in a spiritual world is like.

In a world dominated by the spirit, being wealthy would no longer be the most important goal in life. This will instead be replaced by sharing wealth and resources equally so everyone would no longer need to struggle. In a spiritual world, there would be no war or arbitrary killings, since greed, hatred, prejudice, and fear would no longer dominate our every action; instead, sharing, compassion, and love would replace the current values that are and have dominated the world for millennia. Though many will think living this way is not possible, I assure you it is. This is especially true if we start by teaching our youngest children to be open to the infinite possibility's life has to offer and if they are brought up in a positive way, knowing compassion and empathy rather than fear and hate.

Though it is much easier to instill a positive view of life when children are young, it is possible to change the direction of your life when you are older as well; that is, to learn to approach life in a positive rather than a negative way. To do this later in life, however, is much more difficult and will require challenging many of the false beliefs you were taught when you were growing up. If you commit to positively changing your view of life, you will begin the journey to free your spirit guide and Awaken, so its positive messages may once again be heard more clearly.

If you decide, as I pray you do, to take this journey, it will not be easy or quick. By beginning to free your spirit guide from its imprisonment within you, you will begin to experience and deeply feel many difficult emotions, as well as stress, anxiety, and many other negative emotions as well. When the self alone dominated your life, everything in your world made sense. By simply following all you learned growing up, not challenging what you were taught

43

and blindly following what you were expected to do, you became one of the masses, destined to lead a mediocre life. However, as soon as you begin to question what you learned, the conflict within, caused by the reemergence of the spirit guide, will begin to change your life forever.

Once you decide to do this and begin to awaken, there is no turning back. This conflict will continue for the rest of your life and will result in two things happening: your life will initially get worse and then it will get much better. At first, it will get worse as you unlearn and begin to question if anything you were taught while you were growing up was important or true. You may begin to question your religion, job, possessions, friendships, marriage, and everything else you once believed in. As you do this, the self will try to reassert itself as the dominate guide in your life and, when this happens, you will experience anxiety and stress.

After this initial reaction though, things will get better. Everything will improve after you become enlightened by accepting the guidance of your spirit guide and understanding that little you were taught throughout your life was true. When this happens, though the self will still remain, it will now be relegated to a supportive role in your life. This will allow the spirit guide to fulfill its destiny by becoming the primary focus of your thoughts and energies.

Once you awaken, the road to enlightenment may be very long. For some, it may take years, or may never happen at all. For them, the struggle will be great, but I assure you the journey is worth it. This is the reason you are alive, the meaning of your life and the purpose, we, the spirit guides, who accompany you in life, are here to help you with.

It will take a leap of faith though, to begin this journey by embracing the spirit guide over the self; often, you have no choice. At some point in your life, you may develop an overwhelming feeling something is wrong. Though everything appears to be going well in your life, you are successful and fulfilled the goals you had for your life, this feeling will simply not go away. It is during this time the first cracks in the wall protecting you throughout your life appear as you begin to question your existence and the reason you are alive. You begin to think there must be more to life. To try to fill that void within, you begin to reexamine your life and question the things you once believed were true. Though your life may have been very successful, you start to wonder why you are feeling this way, beginning to feel uneasy and anxious as the uncertainty of what is happening to you causes confusion. Finally, you reach a point of no return, one where you must confront this void, regardless of the outcome. This is the beginning of an awakening, the start of a journey to try to understand what is happening to you. From this point on, nothing will ever be the same. You know this is a journey you must make; one that will change your life forever.

You will begin to question everything you know, believe to be true, and do in life. Everyone you know, including your friends, acquaintances, and family, will be seen differently. The commonalities you once had with others may no longer exist and you may find your relationships changing dramatically.

Your beliefs about the world will change as well. Whereas before you were only concerned about your success and your family, ignoring others who were not as successful as you, now, you begin to clearly see many of the problems and struggles others are having and want to do something to help them. You can no longer ignore these problems, knowing you must do something to make things better.

Before you awoke, your job and the amount of money you made were very important to you; afterwards, however, you may begin to question not only whether you are happy in your job, but also whether the amount of money you are making is really that important. You may even decide to quit your job, taking a different job that pays less, but allows you to be happy at work and help other people at the same time.

After you awake, you begin to reevaluate your entire life; the one certainty is nothing will stay the same. Your relationships will deepen and become more spiritual. Though this change is very good, it may cause you to reconsider whether you want your old relationships to continue. You will also look at the world differently. As your negative view of life begins to change to a positive one, instead of benignly accepting the inequalities in life, you begin to wonder if there is anything you can do to help bring change. Before, you were only concerned you were not poor, homeless, or hungry; you now wonder whether there is anything you can do to help those who are.

Instead of seeing only the worse in people, you will now begin to see the good in others. Instead of darkness, you will see light, instead of helplessness, you will want to help others, and instead of accepting living in a world of fear, you will want to help change the world so others may live in a world of love, compassion, and hope instead.

The Eyes You See the World Through

Look at the world. Do you see an uncaring world in disarray or a world of endless possibilities? How you view the world and others depend on the eyes you see it through.

If you accept all you were taught about living in a self-centered world, it will indeed be a dark place; its shaded colors muted by an array of impure hues.

If, however, the world is seen instead through your loving spirit within, your vision will become clear, revealing the unlimited potential life has always offered.

Chapter 9:
Living in a World of Light

A

ll spirit guides have infinite knowledge, not only about this world, but the universe as well. Before I talk about the universe though, it is important to finish our discussion about the world I currently am on. The spirit guide is not only present in other people, but also in everything that has life; this includes animals, plants, and other forms of life as well. The spirit guide believes in treating all life and the earth with respect. As such, it helps us realize, though we may be the dominant species on this planet, we are no better or more important than any other form of life. Every life has a spirit guide; we all share this planet together. It must be understood, only by recognizing and respecting these spirit guides' journeys as well, will all our journeys through life on this planet be successful.

I would like to tell you what living in a world not dominated by the self is like; that is, living in a world of light, rather than darkness. Living in a world of light is quite different to how life is being lived now and throughout history. In a world of light, the path of the spirit guide is preeminent. Peace, hope, compassion, and love are abundant in such a world, as well as many other positive qualities and emotions. Here, there is no war, senseless killing, prejudice, or inequity. Instead, there is respect for all life; each life is considered special and important. No one is thought to be better than another and all resources are equally shared, including among all other forms of life. Though the self will always be present, the messages from the spirit guide are clearly heard and supersede its messages. The overwhelming stresses and burdens of life are mitigated, as there would be enough food and shelter for everyone, allowing the pursuit of higher spiritual endeavors. Money would have little sway in this world as greed would no longer exist, allowing each of us to help make others' journey easier. Fear and hate would no longer be concerns, being replaced by trust and love. Instead of concern only for ourselves, everyone's success would take precedence.

This is what the world can and should be like. It is hard for me and other spirit guides to understand, knowing all this, why you would choose to continue down the current destructive path the world is on, instead of choosing the spiritual path you were meant to pursue. In order to clearly see how it is different from living in a world of darkness, it is necessary to first talk about what living in a dark world is like. To describe what this world is like, you need only read the newspapers or watch the news.

In a world of darkness, daily challenges and struggles are constantly present. Instead of helping each other, as we are meant to, each person has accepted the view of the self, primarily concerned with themselves, rather than their fellow travelers; and instead of viewing the world as a loving, caring place to live, it is seen as dangerous and competitive. Every day, we read about mass killings, the effects of climate change, hate, fear, greed, and many other negatively triggered events as well. Living this way represents the worst of who we are; unfortunately, this is not only the world of today, but the world throughout most of history as well.

Amara's life was similar to many others. I, Bodhi, introduced myself to her after she was conceived within her mother's womb; for the next nine months, Amara was taught about the spiritual path through life she was being born to pursue. Before she was born, she knew only light. It was not until after Amara was born, just as everyone else, she developed a self that would accompany her through her life as well. And, as it was for everyone else, I too had to compete with her self, so my messages of love and hope could be heard.

With the birth of her self, she was exposed to darkness. The darkness I am talking about are all the false, isolating, negative things Amara learned and was exposed to during her life. The more Amara accepted these false truths, the less bright her light was to shine. Before she was born, her light, as are all other lights, was blinding. As she began her life, though, her light dimmed a little more each day.

My job as a spirit guide is quite difficult and frustrating. Each time, as I watched Amara learn things leading her down a false path, I unsuccessfully tried to redirect her to follow my path. The older she got, and the more she believed what she learned was true, the harder my job became. Each day, her light became a little dimmer, and the path I sought her to follow became a little harder for her to find.

The first five years of Amara's life were the hardest. She was exposed to and learned much from her parents, relatives, brother and sister, minister, the books read to her, movies, tv, and the internet, where she played games and watched videos on her children's tablet. Amara was a typical child, readily absorbing and believing everything she saw and was taught. She wanted to please her parents and would try to do everything they asked her to. She learned how to act and treat others, as well as all the other things expected of her. As a young child does, she believed and internalized everything, and by the time she began school, the bright light she was born with had been significantly dimmed. Her light would further darken periodically during her life, though not as much or quickly as it did during her earliest formative years.

Imagine what life could be like, if a child's light was able to remain bright as they learn the norms of society and how to survive in the world. If this would happen, how we view life and treat others would change forever. The brighter the light remains, especially after the early formative years of life, the easier and more meaningful that child's life will be.

Amara's parents did a fairly good job during her earliest years. As they were teaching her the norms of society and what was expected of her, they mostly emphasized the positive aspects of life. She was brought up knowing the importance of each life and that sharing, empathy, and compassion were good qualities she should always strive for. She was taught to see the best in every person and to treat each with respect. Amara was raised to have a good heart, accepting neither prejudice, fear, nor hate in how her life should be led. Instead, she was taught to see the light within each life and the unconditional love we are all meant to share with each other.

Though Amara and I did not always have a smooth journey through life together, it was far easier than many others because of how her parents socialized and brought her up to recognize the spiritual path during her earliest years of her life. She would still wander off my path, however, at different times in her life; sometimes, she would totally get lost, but she was always able to find her bearings again and return to the loving path we are all meant to follow. She was always encouraged to be a positive person and to care about others. Because of this, Amara's light, though it dimmed slightly, always remained much brighter than others her age. Her struggles through life, therefore, were far fewer.

Even with everything Amara had going for her, it still took many years before she was finally able to clearly hear my voice once more. After all, it is much easier to simply be and act like everyone else; all Amara wanted was to be liked and have friends, as we all do. And so, at times, she lost her way when she was in school, growing up, and following the crowd. She was exposed to others who were prejudiced, hateful, and said mean things to weaker children, bullying them simply to make themselves feel better. Though I tried to keep Amara from acting this way, sometimes, in order to be liked, she simply relented and joined in. Luckily though, she soon realized when she did these things, she felt awful; eventually, she found the strength to stop. Though her light did begin to dim during this time, it did not remain so for long.

For the rest of Amara's life, her light continued to shine brighter than others, as she would try to always see the best in the world. Though the brightness of her light never returned to its pure brilliance before she was born, it did remain quite bright, illuminating her spirit within for all to see.

The journey through life we all take requires us to move from a learned self-centered negative view of life to a positive view of life and from an egoistic world to an altruistic one. Though Amara's journey was unique for her, as it is for all of us, it was not unusual. The blinding light we are first born with will never return. It is only a question of how dull the light will become and how much brightness we can restore during our lifetime. That is the journey we are meant to take. It is my hope, as you read this book, your light may again begin to shine brighter, so you too may follow the path of unconditional love we are all meant to pursue.

Darkness and Light

Darkness is not within. It comes from the self-centered world around us and is internalized. Within there is only light. Darkness, learned after we are born, dominates the views and actions of most, causing many of the man-made problems in the world. Though darkness will always remain throughout our life, it need not control our choices.

It is only when we allow light to direct our actions, becoming our primary guide in life, the world may finally evolve, allowing our children to grow up in a world of peace rather than war, tolerance rather than prejudice, and love rather than hate.

Chapter 10:
What is Success in Life?

I have already briefly spoken about the differences between the self and spirit guide when it comes to defining what a successful life is; these differences could not be more pronounced or have a more meaningful effect on the world in which we live. I think it is important though, to examine this further, so you may make a more informed decision as to the path through life you wish to take in order to live a successful life.

When you are conceived, a spirit guide enters your body, which is simply a shell containing our essence or energy force. It matters little what that body looks like or if the shell is a person, animal, plant, or some other form of life. Since all spirit guides have the same goal, to help each life grow to its full potential, no one life is considered better or more important than another. Regardless of what form that life has taken, in our eyes, all life is considered equal and must be treated with respect and compassion.

Unfortunately, as Amara and others grew up, this is not what they learned. Not only were they to learn they were different and better than others like them, due to any combination of their characteristics, but they also learned they were superior to all other forms of life as well. As children, they believed what they were taught and, therefore, developed a view of the world where others who were different from them, as well as all other life forms, did not need to be treated as equals or with respect. As the self asserted its superiority, the world, and all life on it suffered greatly. Animals and other forms of life were disregarded, killed, and abused with abandon by the dominant species on this planet, even though they, with a spirit guide within them, had as much right to existence and life as we did.

The result of this is chaos, confusion, and numerous hardships, which may be observed in every part of the world. While living this way, is it possible to have a successful life? If success is defined as being able to live a good life, having a lot of money and material things, then perhaps our lives are successful. But this is what the self hopes you will believe. Success in life, according to the self, can be attained by following the rules and guidelines we were taught while we were growing up. We were told having a prestigious job, money, a family, and material possessions will mean our life is successful. We were also told, when we have all these things, not only will we find success in the world, but happiness as well. Though all this may appear to be true, I am here to tell you nothing could be further from the truth. While this is the accepted definition of success, it is also the cause of much of the misery and unhappiness you witness and hear about.

The other definition of success, the one I am about to reveal to you, is quite different. To the spirit guide, success is simply defined as everyone succeeding in life, not just yourself. In this view of success, everything is shared equally. Money no longer dominates our thoughts and actions; it is replaced instead by fairness and equality for all life. Greed, anger, fear, and apathy are instead replaced by love, compassion, and the sincere desire to help others. Thus, a successful life is defined as a life in which the burdens so many experience throughout their lives are shared and lessened by working together.

Picture a future world where success is shared by all. A world where competition, fear, hate, and the desire to outdo others no longer dominate our every thought; a world where food is equally shared, and illnesses treated despite their costs. This is surely a world where there is no homelessness, war, senseless death, or any of the many other problems plaguing our world today and throughout history. If this definition of success were accepted, there would no longer be a need to compete or prove we are better than or superior to another.

To live a successful life, you do not have to reach old age. Too many think their life will be successful if they accomplish all the goals they learned about as they were growing up and live to an elderly age. If you have a family, wealth, material possessions, grow old, and have all the other things we know and were taught will make you successful, then you may consider your life successful. I am here to remind you, though it may be nice to have all these things, they do not define what a successful life truly is.

Given what I have told you, a successful life may even be lived by a small child. Life is so unpredictable; each of us may die at any time and any age. An act of nature, such as a tornado, tsunami, hurricane, earthquake, can end life in an instant. Also, living in a violent unpredictable world, death may come at the hands of another or from an accident. It is therefore a good idea to live each day fully with love.

It is not how long you live or what you acquire when you are alive that determines if your life is successful. Rather, a life is successful if you are able to embrace your true destiny, by accepting, hearing, and sharing the messages of your spirit guide within. I have met hundred-year-olds who have everything, yet whose lives were not successful. I have also met ten-year-old's who were able to tap into the messages of their spirit guide at a very young age and, simply by sharing this with others, had already led a very successful life. By being yourself and sharing your love, compassion, empathy, and kindness with others, the awakening of your spirit guide and enlightenment can come at any time and at any age. And with enlightenment, you will have led a successful life.

There is a choice you must make. By accepting the norms and definition of success you are taught, your life will never be whole. Instead, you will become one of many who struggle through life, never truly finding inner peace or happiness. You may believe you are happy and have led a successful life if you have achieved your self-centered goals in life. However, this untruth, propagated by the self, will eventually only lead to disappointment and a life led without meaning. Though you may not understand this until you review your life, as we all do when death is imminent, it is not too late to make significant changes before then.

In writing this book, it is my hope you will begin to reevaluate your life now, awaken, and redefine success as seen through my eyes. If you are willing to do this, I encourage you to take the path less traveled, the spiritual path you are meant to take, rather than the path you were taught to believe you must follow as you were growing up.

Living a Successful Life

Is success living to an old age, making a lot of money, having a prestigious job, a family, big house, and being able to do the best things life has to offer? Many in the world, believing this self-centered definition of success, though they may become successful in life, if their success is not selflessly shared to help others become successful as well, then their life was led without meaning or purpose.

There is another definition of success though, one much less recognized. Money, material possessions, or anything else found in the world is not necessary when following this path. By selflessly sharing our inherent wisdom and unconditional love, our spirit, with all others, our life will have been successful and we will have understood the genuine purpose for our life's journey.

Chapter 11:
Don't Sweat the Small Stuff

T he self causes us to worry so much about everything in our life we become paralyzed with fear. We worry to the point we are barely able to function each day. Though we do need to be concerned about food, shelter, safety, our family, and health, nothing else is really that important. In fact, I would say, everything else should be considered small stuff.

Does it really matter if we are wealthy, able to buy nice things, or travel the world? Are these things necessary to be able to enjoy life? If you believe in the messages from the self, then the answer to these questions is undoubtably yes. If, however, you have begun to awaken, you may begin to realize they aren't really that important after all.

We stress over everything in our lives. In reality though, except for the few things I mentioned, nothing is really that important. We all want to be happy and are ingrained with images of what we learned that would look like as we were growing up. We are taught to believe happiness may only be found in the self-centered world or through being with another person. Though this happiness may seem real to you, it is an illusion, often temporary, perpetrated by the self, to convince you of its point of view.

In truth though, none of these things will ever bring true happiness or meaning to your life. Though you may feel happy if you do or have these things, the happiness is fleeting and will often disappear when the next challenge in life presents itself.

Almost everything we are taught is important is small stuff; it simply does not matter. Once your basic needs for survival are taken care of, nothing else is truly important; in fact, everything else should be considered small stuff. True happiness, love, meaning, and understanding can only come from within, where it has always been. It is important to find these things there first, then to share them. It is only after you have begun to awaken, will you be able to find what you are looking for in the world. If you do not first look within, the answers to finding real happiness, inner peace, and love will never be found.

By accepting the false path in life, learned from the self, though you may live to an old age, the life you will have led will be shallow and superficial. When this happens, a spirit guide has failed. Though the spirit guide has always been there, the messages of love and hope it has constantly been trying to deliver were not heard. Instead, the messages were lost, muted in the chaos of the world. It is sad when this happens, seeing so much wasted time pursing an artificial, self-centered path through life, instead of the loving path we are all meant to take.

It does not need to be this way though. The reason I am writing this book is to let you know you do not need to wait until the end of your life to understand how life is meant to be lived. It can be discovered much earlier simply by accepting and listening to the messages that I, and all other spirit guides, have been trying to get you to hear throughout your life. You will awaken when you begin to hear these messages. You will become enlightened when you accept them as the truth.

When this happens, your definition of small stuff will be changed forever. Almost everything you once thought was important will no longer be meaningful. The money, big house, fast cars, trips around the world, and the many nice things you own will seem small and petty. The things you felt made you happy and defined your success in life will no longer be important. The false path in life, the path of the self you have pursued throughout your life, will begin to fade away, redirecting you to the spiritual path your spirit guide has tried to have you follow instead. It is unfortunate most will never hear or understand this message during their lifetime, or they will only hear it near the end of their life. Simply take a look at the world today and throughout humanity's reign on earth to see the result of this.

I want to show you what the world could be like if the messages from the spirit guide could not only be heard much earlier in life, but also by all others. In this world, all material things would be considered small stuff. Instead of living in a competitive, cutthroat world, as we do now, everything would be shared for the benefit of all. There would no longer be hunger, homelessness, or climate change, since greed and avarice would not exist. We would help each other through the difficulties life may present, rather than being only concerned for our family and ourselves.

Many illnesses, especially psychiatric illnesses, would lessen, as the underlying cause of these afflictions, the conflicting messages we receive from the self and spirit guide, would no longer trigger the emotional distress that so often leads to stress, anxiety, and depression. Instead, both of these messages, which would still be present, would be better understood and accepted. The learned messages from the self would remain to help us survive in the world, but would no longer dominate our lives, replaced by the messages from the spirit guide instead, now clearly heard and understood.

This is the world we are meant to live in, a world where the travails and worries of life are equally shared. In this world, everything would be considered small stuff. Worries such as hunger, homelessness, or safety would no longer be present; they simply would cease to exist since everyone would help and respect each other.

The planet I am now on is a very fractured dangerous place to live, but it does not need to be. Though it has always been this way, not only is change possible, but it is absolutely necessary. We are at a crossroads where the future of all life must be decided. There is no more time to hope for this change to occur at its own pace. If it does not take place, if a fundamental shift of our consciousness does not begin now, everything will be considered small stuff, since all life on this planet may simply cease to exist.

What is Important in Life?

The time we have left as we approach death is an interesting time in life. Many things, once thought to be important, no longer are. We begin to realize life really is not that complicated or complex; rather, it is quite simple.

The money, material possessions, job we had, and almost everything else we once thought defined what a successful life is, no longer matter. Nothing will accompany us when we die. We finally realize none of those things are, or ever were important.

Do not wait until the end of your life to decide what is truly important. To discover what is important, close your eyes, silence your mind, and listen to the quiet messages in between your racing thoughts.

Chapter 12:
Happiness and Love

W
e all want to be happy and find love. The real question that needs to be asked is: how do we find happiness and love? More importantly, what are they? These are questions asked throughout history, but few have truly found the answers.

We are taught from a very young age what happiness and love are. We are told we will find them if we follow the examples of what we see, read about, and learn from others. But these examples are all artificial and meaningless; they are defined by what we learn, rather than what we inherently know to be true. The mistake we all make is implicitly believing what we are taught and not questioning if it is true or not. We, therefore, spend our lives pursuing this fallacy, trying to duplicate what we learned for ourselves. Even if we are able to do this though, and find happiness and love as others did, we often find there is still something missing; for this type of happiness and love is fleeting, like the wind and rain after a storm passes.

How many people do you know or have heard of, have everything? They have wealth, fame, a prestigious job, family, and everything else that defines success in life, yet they are miserable, unhappy, depressed, unloved, and alone. If happiness and love are defined by what we have and accumulate in our lives, then it simply does not make sense they would feel this way. It is interesting how a successful person, such as an actor or musician, surrounded by thousands of people, can be unhappy and alone, yet it is not as unusual as you may think. By looking for their answers to finding happiness and love from their celebrity and wealth, all they may find instead is emptiness. To be able to find true happiness and love in life, one must first make peace with the spiritual part of your life before you will be able to find it in the world around you. If this is not done, any happiness and love you find will often be temporary and artificial. It is important to find yourself first before sharing the part of you, your spirit guide, that makes you special and unique, with others. Only then will true happiness and love no longer be elusive.

This is the mistake so many make throughout their lives. Instead of seeking answers first from within, where their spirit guide is, they only look for their answers in the external world or in being with others. They therefore struggle all their lives, searching for that they will never be able to find. If, however, you first look within, you will find the answers you seek and then be able to confront the false path you were taught to believe.

You do not have to be famous or wealthy to find happiness and love. Anyone can find these things at any time during their life, but there are no shortcuts. We each need to do the work, confront the false beliefs we have been taught and reconnect with our spirit guide first, before the inner peace we are looking for can be found. This may be a very long lonely journey; I assure you it will not be easy. The self, which represents everything you not only were taught, but believe as well, will fight by doing everything it can to make this change as difficult as possible. The harder you work to change the direction of your life, the more uneasy and unsettled you will feel.

The battle, between what you have learned and what you inherently know to be true, may be debilitating. Many who embark on this journey to change the fundamental way they view life are stressed, anxious, depressed, or develop numerous other ailments, which are inflicted by the self in its attempt to force you to stop. Also, the internal strife, resulting from this journey, will cause numerous difficulties in your personal life as well. It will become increasingly difficult to simply accept the world as it is and the many misdirected people who live in it. This will not only include your acquaintances, but may include your family and friends as well. The pettiness of those who have not yet begun their journey, or those who began it and simply gave up, will overwhelm you.

After you awaken, you may find you have little in common with those closest to you, as they follow the easier path through life, the traditional path they were taught. You may also find you no longer want to participate in the many superficial games in life played every day. As you become more isolated, by reevaluating the direction you want your life to take, the world you now see will begin to change. You begin not only to notice the struggles and challenges in the world differently, but you also begin to want to ease these challenges for others as well. This change is altruistic; it is not a result of hoping to gain wealth or material possessions, but rather it stems from an inherent desire to share and help others.

Once this journey begins, there is no turning back. The only thing I can guarantee you is it will be difficult, long, lonely, and will disrupt your entire life. This journey becomes especially challenging if all, some, or most of those in your life do not take up the journey with you. As you begin to change, not only will you find it more difficult to be around them, but also, they may find it hard to be around you as well. With this change, you will become a different person. The many superficial games and opinions of those who have not chosen to be on your new path will no longer interest you. The way you evaluate and see the world will be through new eyes and, because of this, nothing will ever look the same, and everyone you know will be seen in a different light as well.

There have been some people throughout history who had very little, yet who have led very successful, happy lives. The reason they were able to do this was because they understood everything I am telling you and were able to awaken and become enlightened. They awoke when they began to understand something was missing in their life and they realized where to find it. They became enlightened when they fully accepted not only the presence of their spirit guide, but also accepted its direction and beliefs as well. At that moment, everything made sense to them. An inner peace, an aura of calm understanding, surrounded their very being as their lives changed forever. The disguises others wore faded away, the negativity of life disappeared, and the desire to improve the world, by helping others find their true path, became overwhelming. The false paths of life so many others pursued, and they once followed, became crystal clear. The light now surrounding them began to shine brighter, as it overshadowed the darkened energy fields that once encircled them. Everywhere they look there is darkness; those who have completed their journey try desperately to change things by shining a light on the darkness. They eventually realize though, nothing will truly change until others are willing to take the journey they just completed to find, listen to, and accept the messages from their spirit guide as well.

The reason this begins to happen when you are awakened is because your definition of happiness and love will now be different than it was before. For others happiness and love will still come from the world; yours, however, will now come from within. Though you will attempt to convince your friends and

63

family to make the journey to enlightenment with you, you will find that fear will often prevent them from even trying. It will not be until they are ready that they too will begin to hear the whispers of their own spirit guide; it will only be then, they may try to change the direction of their life as well. After all, seeing how difficult the journey is, and how much stress and anxiety are associated with it, it is not hard to imagine why someone would choose not to face their fear, simply continuing to live their life in the superficial world they have always known. It is easier to not take this journey, but I assure you, the journey is worth it.

Finding Love and Happiness

We search the world to find love and happiness. Though we may believe we have found them, often they are temporary, fleeting, like a passing storms rain.

These things may not be found in a self-centered world. To find genuine love and happiness, look within, then selflessly share your love and happiness to help others find them in their life as well.

Chapter 13:
Life in the Universe

T

o try to put all this into a much broader perspective, I am going to reveal to you something many of you have suspected, but did not actually know for sure: life is not restricted to this planet. There are about two trillion galaxies, one centillion stars, and up to ten quintillion planets in the universe. Given those amazing statistics, I think the question needing to be asked is: how could there not be life elsewhere?

What happens when we die? Throughout millennia, people have sought the answer to this question. There are some who do not believe in my existence or the existence of god. This group of people believe death means the end to their existence. Most others though, believe there is something else after we die.

Death is not something that should be feared; rather, it is the beginning of a new adventure. Many different religions have attempted to describe what happens after we die. They talk of heaven and hell, reincarnation and so many other theories I simply cannot discuss each at this time. Instead, I would simply like to tell you what it is really like.

When you die, only your physical body perishes; the shell that I and all other spirit guides were born into, ceases to exist. Just as the self begins its existence when you are born, it too dies when your body does as well. I, however, and all other spirit guides, are eternal and never perish. It does not matter what kind of life we were joined with, be it person, animal, plant, or any other form of life found throughout the great expanse of the universe. Upon death, we simply join others like us in a different realm or plane of existence, existing at a higher frequency; we lack a body or form, possessing instead an energy field surrounding our essence. It is here we remain until we are once again called upon as spirit guides to accompany a new life.

You may find it interesting, just as there are one centillion stars in the universe, there are at least as many spirit guides as well. If you consider all life, including animals and plants, having their own spirit guide and that life is not isolated to our small planet in the enormous universe, then perhaps you may understand why so many of us exist.

Though we are many, as our essence, which is surrounded by an energy sphere, touches one another, we actually become one. Since the self does not exist after death, all that is felt here is unconditional love. If there is a definition of god, it would be the totality of all spirit guides, connected to each other by their proximity and, therefore, existing as one entity. This one entity, present in an alternate plane of existence, may be considered to be god. To take this discussion one step further, every single spirit guide would therefore represent a piece or part of god. And since there is a spirit guide within everyone and everything that has life, there is a part or piece of god within every life as well.

All life is interconnected. Just as the energy field of all spirit guides touch in the alternate plane they exist in, and thus communicate with each other, while they accompany a life through its journey, there is still a connection between them that is inherent and experienced. This may be difficult to understand, but all life is linked together by the spirit within; all life is one. What happens to any one life affects the universe itself. Each life has a purpose and is meaningful. By abruptly ending a life, everything in the universe is affected. Though the effect may be infinitesimal, the balance of the universe will still be altered.

It is not my intention to confuse you, so I hope you will take the opportunity to really think about what I have told you. Knowing this planet is but a tiny speck in the multitude of light in the universe, puts all our small insignificant problems into perspective. We have convinced ourselves of our supreme importance and intelligence, but are we truly so? Are we any more important than another person, animal, plant, or the many billions of other life forms on the quintillions of planets in the universe? Though your life is important, it is not any more important or superior to any other.

Many people are awakening, beginning to hear and listen to the messages within. However, it is only with enlightenment the path of the self may be permanently altered, becoming subservient to the gentle loving path of the spirit guide instead. We, the spirit guides hope, as this change in perspective increases in the world, it will radically change the world, allowing it to evolve to a higher level of consciousness. This change must not only be made on this planet, but throughout the universe as well. With the advancement of space travel, people on this world will soon begin visiting other planets. On some of these planets, they will find life. Many life forms in the universe have already spiritually evolved; they gave up the primitive, self-centered impulses so prevalent here, long ago. They understand and follow the shared path of their spirit guides, their world living in peace, harmony, and love. It is on these other planets, where life not only already exists but has evolved, the results of living a spiritual life can readily be seen.

On many of these worlds, some on which I have been a spirit guide in the past, the spiritual evolution has already taken place. On these worlds, there is no war, killing, greed, anger, hate, prejudice, or fear. These antiquated traits were eradicated long ago and no longer have a place in their society. Everything is shared equally; respect for all life is universal and the voice of the spirit guide is clearly heard and listened to by all. This is how life is meant to be lived. It is a life where peace, happiness, and love dominate, and the self, though present as well, has minimal influence.

For a spirit guide, life is wonderful on these planets as our voices are easily heard and accepted. Clearly, life on the planet I am currently on, is much more challenging. Here, I face the daily struggle of having my voice recognized. Instead of this planet evolving, it is the self that has evolved instead. And with the elevation of the self, a world of fear and hate emerged.

It is not too late to alter the future, but radical change will be necessary. Just as the other worlds I had previously been on evolved, so must this world. If, during this evolution, the self remains dominant, life on this planet will soon become a small footnote in the history of the universe. If, however, a Darwinian evolution occurs, where the supremacy of the self becomes subservient, being replaced by a more dominant spiritual species, then the evolution of mankind will finally truly begin. Only then may they be able to join the fraternity of life on the many other inhabited evolved planets throughout the universe.

It really is very simple. There is a stark choice that must be made; time is quickly running out to make it: evolution or extinction. It is my hope those on this planet choose wisely.

Will Life on Earth be Missed Once it is Gone?

There are two trillion galaxies in the known universe, each one containing billions upon billions of stars. Each one of those stars may have many planets in orbit around them. There, therefore, may be quintillions of planets in the universe.

Will life on earth be missed once it is gone? No. Life will continue undeterred elsewhere. Our destruction, all but assured if we continue to follow the self-centered path we have always pursued, will barely cause a tiny ripple in space. There is little time left to change this preordained future.

Only by sincerely caring about each other and the planet that sustains us, may we begin to mitigate the many man-made destructive challenges humanity has inflicted on our world, and allow our planet and all who inhabit it, begin to heal.

Chapter 14:
Lessons in Life

T here are many lessons in life that should be taken from this book. The primary lesson, however, is: it is not too late to make the necessary changes so desperately needed. These changes though, must begin soon. The future will ultimately be determined by the next generation of children, but the changes needing to be made must not wait until then to begin. They must begin right now. Unless a philosophical change in direction is adopted, shifting the emphasis of life from a self-centered focus to a collective spiritual one, the changes necessary will be ineffective. Instead, they will fail, as all other efforts to improve the destiny of humanity, have failed in the past.

The answer does not rest with religion or with anything else found or believed in the world. Instead, it rests with an evolution in our thoughts and destiny as to what our future will be. Adopting the spiritual path, awakening as many as possible, with the ultimate goal of enlightenment, must be the path forward that is pursued. Hopefully, this will allow the newest generation of children enough time to mature and change the direction of the planet before it is too late. These children must be brought up with positive light and values, respecting all life and their importance in the universe. It is these children that will ultimately save the planet; in the meantime though, we must help extend the time available to them until they grow up and assume positions of influence in society. Everyone must work to adopt this new path in life, or life will become unsustainable.

In retrospect, I should have written this book two or three millennia ago in order to prevent the situation from deteriorating as badly as it has. With how life was at that time, however, I am not sure success would have been much better.

There is a choice that must be made: to continue along the same path of the self or to alter that path and accept the direction of the spirit guide instead. If you choose to follow the former path, then the lessons of history, that should have been learned, will be lost and nothing will change. The death, brutality, struggle, and wars of the past will go unchanged, as greed and fear will continue to dominate our choices and actions. If, however, you believe life can be better than this, please join me, and my fellow spirit guides, in choosing the latter path, beginning a spiritual evolution that will positively change the direction and future for all life on this planet.

The radical change necessary will challenge and bring into question everything accepted as the norm throughout history. Every belief and dogma must be reviewed, challenging everything we learned and believed to be true. This will be extraordinarily hard to do, but it is absolutely necessary. This is so important, I am taking this extreme action by overtly revealing my existence to you. I did not do this without much consideration; it is being done out of absolute necessity. Time is rapidly running out, necessitating this change to begin now.

I am the first spirit guide to ever write a book. As all spirit guides are connected, we all decided, as one, this drastic action was necessary due to the urgency of the situation on this planet. By exposing the truth in this way to everyone, it is our hope to expedite humanity's spiritual evolution and, by doing so, alter the dangerous future lying ahead for all life on this planet. After Amara awoke and became enlightened, at my urging, she began to write this book. As she sits typing on her computer, my thoughts steadily flow to her. We communicate as if we are one.

This book is only the beginning, however. Each person who has successfully started or completed this journey must now share their wisdom and love as well. There have been many good spiritual books written about those who have become enlightened; it is one way to teach and share with others what you have learned. For others, just being yourself, adopting the loving values and beliefs of the spirit guide wholeheartedly into your life, those you meet will observe your calm peaceful demeanor, wishing to emulate it and therefore, start to approach their life's challenges differently. Such encounters may trigger the awakening process of numerous others, including many who you may barely know.

Awakening, becoming enlightened, and selflessly sharing your spirit guide's innate wisdom and unconditional love to improve the life of others, is the meaning of life; the reason we are born. Life is only successful if everyone succeeds; it was never meant to be lived alone or in isolation.

When spirit guides view today's world, we see a world of greed, dominated by the self, to the detriment of all others. Until this misguided approach to life is radically changed, the future will not be altered. Though this change has begun, due to the increasing dangers and threats to each other and the planet daily, much more must be done. Every action taken without love and compassion must be challenged, regardless of what that action is. It is no longer acceptable to remain silent; this has been done far too long. Evil, resulting from an extreme interpretation of the self, must be aggressively confronted to expose the underlying false messages.

Though the self and spirit guide will be with Amara and everyone else throughout their life, the path you choose through life will determine how your life will be led. You have a choice which path to follow, but the choice is harder to make than you may realize. It is much easier to follow the path of least resistance by not challenging the mores you are taught throughout your life. If you do this, you will live your life asleep, passing without realizing your full potential. You will be just like everyone else; you will be born, live, and die, never understanding the reason you were alive.

The other possibility though, is much more difficult to achieve. It is by challenging everything you learned and were taught throughout your life. Only then may the answers you seek may be found.

It is my hope you will join me, and the other spirit guides, in this endeavor, so life on this planet may finally spiritually evolve, as it is meant to. It is time for the earth to join the other spiritually evolved planets of the universe, becoming one with each other and with all other sentient beings as well.

Hear My Voice
(This last poem is written by Ken's Spirit Guide, Bodhi)

We have watched humanity from its birth squander the incredible gift of life we bestowed on you. The purpose of life is for you to selflessly share your inherent wisdom and unconditional love, present within each, with all others without favor.

Instead, humanity created an alternative path, pursuing only what is best for one, rather than all. Though our directive is to remain silent, allowing humanity to choose its own destiny, as the world rapidly approaches a precipice, we may no longer remain quiet.

To survive, humanity must work together, realizing the original purpose of life. If it does not, continuing on its current path, then we, your spirit guide's within, connecting each life to the other, will have failed in our quest.

Epilogue:

Author's (Ken's) Journey Through Life

I knew since I was a small child the reason I was born was to awaken, become enlightened, and share this knowledge with others. My journey through life, however, to reach these lofty goals, took many unexpected difficult turns. Though I was brought up in a religious family, it did not help me hear the messages from my spirit guide. If anything, religion only further isolated me from my spirit guide, Bodhi, teaching me to accept the self's view of religion and life, instead of his.

I struggled throughout my years trying to understand the reason I was born and the meaning of life. This struggle was the result of a childhood in which the beliefs and values of my self were strongly reinforced and those of my spirit guide mostly forgotten. I finally came to understand religious dogma and its belief in god actually has very little to do with spirituality. I was raised to believe god was someone in heaven, who could be loving or vindictive, depending on the circumstances of whether I listened to him or not. In reality, it was not until after I stopped following a formal religion, I finally was able to embrace spirituality, and with this embrace, I awoke.

Spirituality is the belief there is a piece of god, a spirit guide, within everything that has life, and, because of this, all life is important, equal, and connected. Without the dogma of religion handicapping my views, I was suddenly free to explore this philosophy of life more deeply. Before I could do that, however, I had to confront my self, which was focused and formed when I was a child. It was then, when I was completely overwhelmed by life, my self trapped my spirit guide for most of my life, behind an impenetrable wall built around my heart. Little did I realize it would take the majority of my life before that wall could be destroyed, finally freeing my spirit guide from its prison within.

I also wore a mask for the majority of my life that protected and allowed me to survive in the world. My mask covered my entire face, fitting so tightly no one, not even my family, knew what I really felt. I would always smile, appear happy, though, I would often feel intense anxiety within. This was something I never really understood until I awoke.

For many years, I never let anyone penetrate either my wall or mask. Both of these were formed when I was a small child and were to have a profound effect on the majority of my life. By protecting me from emotional pain, they also isolated me from my family, everyone else in my life, as well as from myself. Absolutely no one could hurt me; I never let anyone get close. The drawback to this, however, is I lived a superficial life, allowing my self to dominate my life completely. Though I had many acquaintances, I had few friends due to my inability to allow anyone to get close enough to know the real me.

For most of my life I lived in fear. I was afraid of being emotionally hurt, as I was when I was a child. I was determined not to let anyone hurt me again. I, therefore, distanced myself from everyone, including my family, allowing them to only see the artificial facade I created to protect me. This superficial life, one devoid of risk or pain, left me alone in a sea of people.

It took many years before the first cracks in my wall formed and before I could loosen the mask I constantly wore. The reason they were so strong and difficult to discard was because how powerful my self became when I was a young child; it actually overwhelmed me for the majority of my life. It is amazing to think about it now. I spent all those wasted years of my life desperately searching for answers in the world, trying to undo and unlearn what I was taught during the earliest years of my life. Though my parents were loving and meant well, they reinforced my self so strongly when I was a child, the bonds holding my spirit guide down felt unbreakable.

I always knew though, since I was little, why I was born. Inherently, my spirit guide desperately tried to change the path the self had me following. Though I have heard of some who became enlightened a few years after they awoke, it took me almost an entire lifetime, and I am still on the path with more to learn and understand.

With Bodhi's help, the bonds of my wall finally shattered completely, freeing Bodhi from his lifelong prison. Also, I was able to rip off and discard the mask I had worn since I was a little child. I thought, when this happened, it would bring me closer to others; it did not. I actually felt more isolated instead. I no longer wanted to play the games other people played anymore. The guilt, anger, fear, and self-centeredness of those I knew, including some members of my family, no longer held any meaning or importance to me. I felt myself drifting away, as I reevaluated everything I thought I knew about life.

After I was clearly able to hear my spirit guide, Bodhi, I realized little I had learned from my self throughout my life was true. I had looked for love and happiness in the job I had, money I made, things I owned, and through my wife and children. Except for the latter, I finally realized none of that was important or would ever allow me to be happy and find meaning in my life.

I am grateful to my self, however, because it did allow me to live in the world, teaching me coping skills, allowing me to survive in life. Though I had everything I wanted in life, I still felt a huge void within. It was a void I could not get rid of until I finally shattered my wall, ripped off my mask, and opened my heart to the possibility's life has to offer. Though my self still remains within me, it has now taken a secondary role in my life, relinquishing its primary role to my spirit guide, Bodhi. This is what enlightenment is. It can be unsettling though. I was vulnerable now, but for the first time since I was a small child, I was also free.

The next thing I had to decide was what to do with this knowledge. For many who have achieved this during their lifetime, it is very tempting to simply withdraw from society. They look at the world and see hate, fear, cruelty, hunger, homelessness, poverty, and greed. Also, they found they no longer had much in common with many others, not wanting to play the games they played anymore; their lives remaining dictated by their self. They came to realize unless their family and friends wanted to take the same journey they did and seek to awaken as well, they would have little left to talk about, as they slowly began to drift away from each other.

I always knew the gift I was destined to receive, the gift of enlightenment, must be shared. I had known my entire life this was my destiny. My journey began after a near death experience when I was ten years old, though it was not until the twilight of my life, I was able to write, with Bodhi's help, nine spiritual books, to try to share this knowledge with others. It is my and Bodhi's hope you will read these books, and by doing so, begin a new adventure, one where you too will awaken and begin on a journey to find enlightenment as well.

Our Journey of Rediscovery

We are all on the same journey of rediscovery, trying to return to the divine path we once knew before we were first born, rather than the path we were taught to accept after we were exposed to the reality of living in an indifferent, self-centered world.

Author's Note:

It is my hope your understanding of awakening, enlightenment, and spirituality has been enhanced by reading 'The Spirit Guide. If it has, could you please take a few minutes to click on the link below to: "Write a Review" and recommend this book on social media and to your friends and family.

https://books2read.com/u/bWJoqM

The Spirit Guide was written to try to awaken and help others who are awakened more fully understand what enlightenment is, so their spiritual journey through life may be more fully realized.

Thank you for taking the time to read:
'The Spirit Guide'. Please consider reading the other three books in this series as well.

I am including an addendum with an assortment of 50 spiritual reflections using metaphor, imagery, and spiritual insight to explore themes of awakening, enlightenment, and the human pursuit of meaning. These reflections are included in Book 1 of Spiritual Reflections. It is my hope you may consider reading the other book in this series as well as you further your search to discover the meaning of life.

Books by Ken Luball

The four Spiritual books in The Awakening Tetralogy:
Today I Am Going to Die: Choices in Life
The Spirit Guide: Journey Through Life
Tranquility: A Village of Hope
The Illusion of Happiness: Choosing Love Over Fear
A Mystical Trilogy: 'Our Search for Meaning' - a series of three books of thoughtful easily understandable spiritual reflections about awakening, enlightenment, spirituality, & the meaning of life.

****

A Spiritual Duology: '*Spiritual Reflections*' - Two books of spiritual reflections using metaphor, imagery, and spiritual insight to explore themes of awakening, enlightenment, and the human pursuit of meaning.

The first three stories in *The Awakening Tetralogy* are written in the first person, following the spiritual journey through life of a child, as they learn the lessons needed during their life to awaken and become enlightened. These books are written in an understandable, interesting, unique narrative, which is both thought-provoking and engaging.

To find links for each of these nine books please visit my website: kenluball.com[1].

Addendum

---

1. http://kenluball.com/?fbclid=IwAR1ig1x0zSJBth8qgyuOPoC1Ynov26InfSRV0cUsnkz3fgAG13FFcnTPJ
01

Addendum:

Spiritual

Reflections

Glossary

Asleep – After we are born we are taught how to survive in the world and what success is. We therefore learn to worry only about our own success and survival in the world, rather than to be concerned about others. This results in living in a self-centered world of prejudice, inequity, and endless struggle. Those who fully believe this are asleep, accepting the status quo as the truth.

Awaken – There may come a time in our life when, despite our success in the world, we begin to question the truth of our self-centered learned beliefs, our ego. When this happens the first quiet messages of the spirit, a piece of god present within every life are sensed, beginning us on an enduring journey to discover meaning in our life.

Ego – The ego is everything we learn, believe, and accept is true after we are born, as we learn how to survive in a self-centered world. Its primary concern is what is best for us; it worries little about others. It also attempts to build up our self-esteem by convincing us of our value in the world.

Enlightenment – The complete acceptance of the spiritual path, allowing the spirit's inherent wisdom and unconditional love to be our primary guide in life. With enlightenment, the ego, our self-centered learned beliefs, assumes a secondary role in our life, no longer influencing the direction of our life choices.

Spirit/ Soul/ God / Higher-Self – An ethereal entity accompanying and inextricably connecting every life to another's. Its purpose is to give our lives meaning by sharing its inherent wisdom and unconditional love to help guide our life's choices.

Spirituality – Spirituality is the belief there is a piece of god, a spirit or soul within every life intimately linking each of us to the other, and, because of this, each life, regardless of our differences, accomplishments, or genus, is important, equal, and connected.

The Butterfly

It is not others who must change.
It is you who must first evolve.
Only then may you begin to
come out of your cocoon
and become a butterfly.

What is Important in Life?

The time we have left as
    we approach death is an
    interesting time in life.
    Many things, once thought to
    be important, no longer are.
    We begin to realize life really
    is not that complicated or complex;
    rather, it is quite simple.
    The money, material possessions,
    job we had, and almost everything
    else we once thought defined what
    a successful life is, no longer matter.
    Nothing will accompany us when we die.
    We finally realize none of those things
    are, or ever were important.
    Do not wait until the end of your
    life to decide what is truly important.
    To discover what is important, close
    your eyes, silence your mind, and
    listen to the quiet messages in
    between your racing thoughts.

Do Not Waste Your Life Living in Fear

If we measure time from the
    beginning of the universe,
    our life passes like a grain
    of sand on a beach or a
    drop of water in an ocean.
    To waste our brief life living
    in fear, believing we are better
    than another, accepting the self-
    centered myths we have been
    taught about our importance
    in the world, masks the
    true purpose of life.
    To live a truly meaningful life,
    we must ignore everything we
    have been taught and believed
    to be true about our importance
    in the world; accepting, though
    we are all different, our
    life is not that significant.
    Every life, regardless of our
    differences, accomplishments,
    or genus, each with a spirit,
    a piece of god within, is,
    and always has been, as
    important as another's.

Mid-Life Crisis

After someone awakens, there is
    often a difficult period of transition.
    That person begins to question
    everything in their life.
    Many people go through a
    mid-life crisis at this time.
    They are confused, questioning
    everything they learned and
    once believed to be true.
    There is a gnawing feeling within
    they may no longer ignore,
    coming from their very core.
    It is their spirit attempting to
    communicate with them, making
    them question the self-centered
    path in life they are on.
    Finally reaching a point no longer
    able to ignore this feeling, they
    have no choice but to make
    changes in their life; they awaken.
    Friendships and relationships might
    fade away, their job may appear
    unsatisfying, as they now may
    have little in common with
    those still asleep, who remained
    trapped in an illusion of reality.
    They begin a journey to find
    meaning in their life; one that
    will lead them to rediscover
    their spirit's inherent wisdom
    and unconditional love,

allowing them to share it to
help others awaken to their
life's genuine purpose as well.

With Awakening Everything Changes

It is all part of the journey.
   Once you awaken, the only
   certainty is your life will
   never be the same and
   there is no turning back.
   Everything in your life will
   change, including your relationships,
   beliefs, and patience for the games
   people play who remain asleep.
   Awakening happens when, sensing
   the first quiet messages from your
   spirit within, you begin to question
   everything you were taught about
   how to succeed and survive
   in a self-centered world.
   Enlightenment though will only
   happen when you truly accept
   everything you learned was untrue.
   The truth has always been within.
   To discover what it is and the
   true reason for your life's journey,
   listen to the silence in between
   your random thoughts, then
   share the wisdom you
   sense from its guidance.

The Splendor of the Whole

We are each like a grain of
    sand on a beach or a drop
    of water in an ocean; part
    of a greater whole, without
    which the beach or
    ocean could not exist.
    It is only when we truly
    understand this, joining all
    the sand and water together
    as one, the splendor of the
    whole may be appreciated.

The River

On top of a tall rocky mountain
    peak covered in snow all year,
    a river begins its long journey
    to an ocean far away, being
    energized by the melting snow.
    Along the way, other steams
    join its trek, as the twisting
    river begins to grow in
    size and straighten its path.
    Many along the river's edge
    use its water to drink and
    grow food for sustenance.
    They also pollute the water
    with waste destroying its
    purity and beauty.
    By the time the river reaches
    the ocean, little is left of what
    it looked like at its beginning.
    We, humanity, are the river.
    We begin our journey at birth,
    pure, knowing only unconditional love.
    As we begin our voyage through
    life though, we are exposed to the
    self-centered beliefs that influence
    and dominate us until our demise.
    Instead of the purity and splendor
    we once knew when we were
    born, our life has slowly decayed.
    By the time we reach the end of
    our journey, reviewing the life we
    had led, many will have regrets.

What once began with beauty
and love, now is unrecognizable.

The Play

On the day we are going to die,
    when the ego, our self-centered
    beliefs, finally surrenders its
    hold on our life, we will understand
    our entire life was a play;
    it was all make-believe.
    We acted our part so well we
    never knew it was not real.
    Life is just an illusion, where we
    all have our bit parts in the play.
    If we follow the script, as we
    learned to do as we are growing
    up, the answers we seek
    about life may elude us.
    It is only when we act outside
    the boundaries of the script and
    awaken, the answers we seek may
    finally begin to reveal themselves.

The Matrix

The matrix is a world where
  most are asleep, living
  in a learned reality
  accepted as the truth.
  Those who remain sleeping
  throughout their lives believe
  success, happiness, and meaning
  may be found in the self-
  centered world; they may not.
  When we first awaken, we start
  to question if those beliefs are true.
  Despite how successful our life
  has been, sensing a voice we
  begin to hear within, the self-
  centered beliefs we once
  unquestionably accepted as the
  truth no longer make sense to us.
  The matrix we once understood
  and accepted as our reality
  begins to dissolve, leaving an
  unrecognizable world in its place.
  Rather than compete against each
  other to survive in the world, we now
  wish to selflessly help others instead.
  Open your heart, see the genuine
  possibility's life offers, allowing
  your matrix to melt away.

The Suitcase

I would like you to picture
    an open suitcase.
    Before we are born, the
    suitcase is empty.
    With our birth, though,
    the self, which is everything
    we learn and believe to be
    true, begins to fill this suitcase up.
    With each interaction we have,
    the suitcase becomes heavier, as
    it begins to become cluttered with
    the baggage we accumulate from
    all the erroneous things we
    have learned during our lives.
    The heavier the suitcase becomes,
    the dimmer our light gets and
    the more we will have to unpack
    when we awaken and begin our
    journey toward enlightenment.
    In the suitcase are all the false
    self-centered truth's learned
    and accepted by the child
    as they are growing up.
    Though it does not take very
    long to fill the suitcase, usually
    during the first five years of life,
    it may take the rest of their life,
    if at all, to find their light again,
    unpack the suitcase and return
    to the inner peace, love, and
    understanding they once knew

before the suitcase began to fill.
Let us all therefore strive to keep
our children's suitcase lighter
during their early years, by raising
them with love, rather than fear,
allowing their light to remain
brighter and their journey through
life easier and more meaningful.

The Seeker

We spend our entire life seeking,
    looking for happiness, love,
    and meaning in our life.
    We search for these throughout
    the world, believing religion,
    money, material possessions,
    having a family, prestigious job,
    or any of the many other things
    we learned would aid our quest.
    Though we may have led a
    successful life, what we are
    searching for may not be
    found in a self-centered world.
    It may only be found within,
    where the answers we have
    sought our entire life, searching
    endlessly for in the world,
    have always been.

The Lie

As soon as we are
    born, the lie begins.
    We are taught about our
    importance in the world and to
    accept its self-centered beliefs.
    We learn those who are famous,
    wealthy, have important jobs, a
    certain skin color, religion, sex,
    or any other comparisons we
    learned defined superiority in
    the world, are better, their lives
    more important than others
    who are different from them.
    Nothing could be
    further from the truth.
    Our egocentric upbring is the
    cause of greed, war, prejudice,
    and many of humanity's other
    harmful beliefs and self-inflicted
    challenges in the world both
    today and throughout history.
    The truth is no one is, or ever has
    been, more important than another.
    Every life, regardless of our differences,
    accomplishments, or genus, each
    with a piece of god, a spirit within,
    is as important as our own, and
    only by equally shepherding the
    resources of our planet, may we
    all survive and live a life of
    genuine purpose and meaning.

The Prism

When we are first born, before
    we are socialized and taught
    what to believe, the light
    refracted through the prism
    of life is pure white.
    This white light emerges due
    to the inherent wisdom and
    unconditional love present
    within each life.
    As we learn how we are
    supposed to act and treat each
    other though, living in a self-
    centered world, the white light
    of the prism is dispersed into
    an infinite number of hues.
    The more we accept and
    believe what we are taught,
    the murkier the reflected
    colors of the rainbow flowing
    through the prism become.
    The darker the light emerging
    from the prism, the more
    challenging our life will become.
    Most of humanity's self-inflicted
    problems and harmful emotions
    experienced around the world,
    both now and throughout history,
    happen when a majority see
    a darkened light emerging
    through the prism of life.
    As we awaken, sensing the first

loving messages from our spirit
within, we begin to question the
truth of what we had been taught.
The colors we now see reflected
through the prism begin to
lighten as we start to reject
much of what we once believed.
The lighter the colors observed on
the other side of the prism the
more peaceful, loving, and
meaningful our life will become.
Though we may never once again
see the pure white color we knew
before we were first born, it
is the journey to rediscover
this white light that is the
genuine reason we are alive.

How Much is a Life Worth?

The going rate for a body,
    including the elements it is
    composed of, is just one dollar.
    Is that what each life is worth?
    Does having wealth, fame, a
    prestigious job, being a certain
    race, religion, sex, or anything
    else differentiating us from each
    other, make one person's life
    worth more than another's?
    These questions must be answered
    by anyone seeking to awaken
    and become enlightened.
    If your answer to these
    questions is yes, your spiritual
    journey has not yet begun.
    If, however, you begin to
    question how much a life is
    worth, wondering if despite
    our differences each life may
    be equally important, then you
    have awoken and begun your
    journey toward enlightenment.

The End of Life

After we have lived our lives,
as we approach death, it is
common to reexamine
how our life went.
Did we live a successful life?
The end of life offers a unique
opportunity to do this, because
at this time, the ego, our learned
self-centered beliefs, loosens its
influence on us, and the spirit
becomes our predominant reviewer.
At this point in the cycle of life,
it no longer matters how much
money we made, the size of the
house we lived in, the job we
had, or anything else associated
with success, as dictated
in the world by the ego.
We are all finally equal
now and we judge our
success through a different
prism: that of the spirit.
When we review our lives,
what we had thought was
success often holds a
different meaning now.
It is at this time, especially
during the last few days of
our life, we come to the
realization what we thought
was important, really was not.
All the material things we
accumulated, friends we had,

places we visited, jobs we
worked, amount of money
we made, or any other comparison
you can think of, which belongs
in the world in which we had
lived, becomes meaningless.
It is at that moment, the moment
where the ego has minimal
control over our actions and
decisions, the true meaning of
life finally becomes evident.
It is then, despite how strongly
the ego may have influenced
our life before, the opportunity
to view our life in a different
way presents itself.
At this time in our life, primarily
viewing our lives through the
eyes of our spirit, we may
find we have many regrets.
We begin to understand the
selfish pleasures in the world we
had sought were not very important.
As death becomes evident, we
finally realize none of that matters.
When we die, unless our culture
is like that of the ancient Egyptians,
our body will be buried or cremated,
and nothing we accumulated during
our lifetime will accompany us.
Our body will then be placed in a
coffin or urn, just like every other
person who dies, regardless of their
stature or their lifetime accomplishments.
At that moment, just before we

die, we finally understand
we truly are all equal.
No one was ever
better than another.
Race, money, prestige,
no longer matter.
As we get closer to our death,
it becomes evident the self-
centered path the ego had us
follow to find success and
happiness may have not
been the right path after all.
The fear, hatred, and prejudice
we once felt are no longer
important to us, not because
we are going to die, but
because it never did matter.

We Are Not Alone

Surrounded by a sea of people,
    I pass many others, barely
    noticing my existence.
    Within, I feel empty, lost,
    afraid of everything, needing
    to prove my worth every day.
    I constantly worry, wanting to
    be happy, successful, be able
    to survive in the world, providing
    everything my family and I need
    to be safe and enjoy the
    best things life has to offer.
    I'm afraid to think too much.
    If I do, I may realize, from the
    moment of our birth until we die,
    we each are alone in the world.
    The journey through life though,
    was never meant to be solitary,
    searching for answers never able
    to be found in a self-centered world.
    To find your answers, to be happy,
    successful, live a meaningful life,
    and not be alone, look within,
    where your spirit, a piece of
    god is present, then selflessly share
    your spirit's innate wisdom and
    unconditional love with all others,
    so they too may be happy,
    successful, and live a
    meaningful life as well.

Inner Voices

We each have two
   voices we hear within.
   One, coming from our mind
   is loud, often misguided,
   telling us what to do and say.
   The words uttered from our
   mind result from what we
   learned in life, determining
   our beliefs, prejudices, and views
   of living in a self-centered world.
   The other voice
   comes from our heart.
   This voice is inherent,
   present within every life.
   Many call this voice our
   spirit or higher-self.
   Selflessly sharing its innate
   wisdom and messages of
   unconditional love to benefit
   others, gives our life meaning.
   Though both voices will remain
   with us throughout our life, we may
   choose which voice to listen to.
   Listen mostly to the softer voice
   quietly whispering its wisdom and
   messages of love, rather than the
   louder chaotic voice from the mind.
   If you do, you will awaken and
   begin an extraordinary journey
   to discover life's genuine purpose.

Look Beyond

When we look at and talk to
        another, what do we see and hear?
    Do we see their appearance, the
    clothes they are wearing, the color
    of their skin, or any of the many
    other traits we judge another by?
    Do we hear just what they are saying,
    the words answering our questions
    or as they tell us their opinion?
    Is there more to someone than
    just what we see and hear?
    Our self-centered opinions,
    often formed when we are young,
    guide most of our interactions
    and how we view the world.
    It is only when we look beyond
    our vison and thoughts, to
    the very soul within another,
    that we may truly know
    their genuine worth.

Who Am I?

Am I the person you see, hear,
  touch, or am I something else?
  Am I the many roles I have
  been assigned by society?
  A father, mother, rich, poor,
  white, black, Asian, European,
  or any of the many other
  designations we are defined as.
  Perhaps I am more than this.
  I, as every life, am a spirit as well.
  Our body is but a shell housing
  who we truly are.
  We are each the same, having
  a spirit, a piece of god within,
  equally alive to experience life.
  Our accomplishments, appearance,
  or any other differences
  between us mean little.
  Who am I?
  I am you and we are all one,
  intimately linked together by
  our spirit within, each alive to
  discover our life's true purpose.

Do No Harm

When we harm another with
    unkind words, take advantage
    of them in any way needing to
    prove we are smarter, more
    important than they are, though
    we may briefly succeed in
    our effort, in reality, the
    injury hurts us both.
    We must always strive to
    help, not harm each other.
    Regardless of the slight, there
    is never a reason to demean another.

Who is Driving Your Car?

When I was born, my car was
    new, pristine in every way.
    I was the driver inherently knowing
    my purpose in life: to follow my
    spirit's inherent wisdom and
    unconditional love, allowing
    it to guide my life choices.
    As I became older though, a passenger
    joined me in my car, when I began
    to accept society's beliefs about life.
    I learned the truth about surviving
    in a self-centered world.
    Slowly, as I became older,
    I discovered I no longer
    was driving my car.
    Instead, I was now the
    passenger: my ego was driving.
    I no longer embraced unconditional
    love as I first did when I was born.
    Instead, I now accepted the countless
    lessons life taught me, understanding
    the many man-made tragedies and
    struggles others endure were inevitable.
    One day, when I was older, depressed,
    unhappy with my life, I began to
    tire being a passenger.
    I started to question if everything I
    had learned in my life was true.
    When I finally realized and accepted
    little of it was, I once again took the
    wheel of my car, changing seats with

the driver, who now accompanied
me in the passenger seat.
As I began to drive my car again,
though it was not as shiny and pristine
as it was when it was new, I was
no longer depressed or unhappy.
Instead, I found genuine inner
peace and meaning, as I once
again was able to embrace and
share my unconditional love,
my spirit, with all others.

A Smile and a Kind Word

Each of us can affect the
    life of another, even briefly.
    Treating others with a smile and
    sincere kindness, not influenced
    by wanting something in return,
    can alter the direction of not only
    one life, but of the world itself.
    This kind-hearted gesture may
    awaken in others an inherent memory
    present within every life; a memory
    we all once knew before we
    were exposed to the chaos from
    living in a self-centered world.
    If enough people begin to selflessly
    share a smile and kind word,
    perhaps the newly awakened
    person we first encountered
    will then share this gesture with
    others, continuing ad infinitum.
    To change the world, perhaps
    we can simply start with being
    nice to each other by sharing
    a smile and a kind word.

The Twilight of Life

As I sit on my porch on a
    cold winter day in the twilight
    of my life, I reflect on what
    is important in life.
    I look at the many struggles others,
    as well as I, had; hunger, homelessness,
    prejudice, inequity, life changing loss
    of job, divorce, illness, death or any
    number of other challenges I
    have witnessed during my life.
    I now understand how unnecessary
    many of these difficulties were.
    They were a result of living in a
    self-centered world, where we
    worry only about ourselves,
    rather than to be sincerely
    concerned for others who
    are struggling as well.
    We need not face life alone.
    We are meant to help each
    other in our time of need,
    understanding every life,
    regardless of our differences,
    is equally important, and only
    together, may we mitigate the
    many self-inflicted problems
    caused by living in an egoistic
    world, allowing us all to survive
    and live a meaningful life full
    of inner peace, enduring love,
    and genuine purpose.

How to Raise a Happy Child

To raise a happy child, bring
    them up to believe in the
    goodness of life, to share
    unselfishly, foster respect
    and love for all others,
    regardless of any differences
    there may be between us.
    Teach our children to find their
    path and happiness in life, not in
    the self-centered world, but from
    their spirit within instead, then to
    selflessly share their spirit's
    innate wisdom and unconditional
    love with all others.

Every Life is Beautiful

It matters not what someone
    looks like: their race, sex, wealth,
    appearance, or anything else
    we may judge them by.
    Every life is unique,
    beautiful in every way.
    Our differences create a
    montage, a mosaic that
    together make us all stronger.
    Despite any insignificant flaws
    we each may have, only by
    embracing our similarities,
    rather than our differences,
    may we truly see the genuine
    beauty within other's.

The Spiritual Journey

The spiritual journey is very
    challenging, long, and often lonely.
    There are a lot of frustrations you
    will encounter as you continue
    to live in a self-centered
    world that remains asleep.
    By embracing the spiritual path,
    selflessly sharing our spirit's inherent
    wisdom and unconditional love, we
    may change the world by awakening
    the spirit within others, beginning
    them on a spiritual journey as well.
    Though the journey is challenging,
    we must not give up.
    For at the end of the spiritual path
    lies inner peace, enduring love,
    and a genuine understanding
    about our life's true purpose.

The Answers

Do not look to others to
    find happiness, meaning,
    and answers about life.
    They will not be found there.
    These must first be found
    within, then selflessly shared,
    without motive or benefit,
    with all others.

The Mask

We learn, often when we are
    young children, how to conceal
    our true emotions behind a mask
    we may wear, becoming very
    adept at hiding almost all our
    feelings from others and,
    often, even from ourselves.
    Masks help us survive in a self-
    centered world, allowing our
    responses to different situations
    to be socially acceptable.
    It is not easy though to
    continually wear a mask.
    The larger the mask and the
    more of our face it covers,
    the greater the problems we
    will have in our life and the
    more stress and anxiety we
    may experience and feel.
    We must all strive to rip off
    the mask preventing us from
    reaching our full potential.
    If we do, allowing our spirit to
    become the primary guide in
    our life, we will be finally be
    able to experience life as
    it was truly meant to be.

The Simple Message We Are Here to Learn

Greed, prejudice, inequity;
    war, hunger, homelessness.
    None of these things and so
    much more need exist today.
    Every man-made problem and
    harmful emotion results from
    accepting the self-centered
    status quo, the belief we are
    better and more deserving
    than another; we are not.
    We are all spirit, each
    with a piece of god within,
    intimately linked to each other.
    Every life, therefore, regardless
    of our differences, is equally
    important, each deserving to
    be helped in their time of need
    and treated with respect
    and unconditional love.
    This is the simple message
    we are here to learn.

Living a Successful Life

Is success living to an old age,
    making a lot of money, having
    a prestigious job, a family, big
    house, and being able to do the
    best things life has to offer?
    Many in the world, believing
    this self-centered definition
    of success, though they may
    become successful in life, if
    their success is not selflessly
    shared to help others become
    successful as well, then
    their life was led without
    meaning or purpose.
    There is another definition
    of success though, one
    much less recognized.
    Money, material possessions,
    or anything else found in the
    world is not necessary when
    following this path.
    By selflessly sharing our inherent
    wisdom and unconditional love,
    our spirit, with all others, our life
    will have been successful and we
    will have understood the genuine
    purpose for our life's journey.

We Are Each Other's Teachers

Every person we meet, regardless
 how brief, affects our life.
 A small part of their spirit,
 their essence, remains with us,
 changing, if only slightly, the
 direction our life will take.
 Each one of us, therefore,
 may change the world by
 sharing our authentic self,
 our spirit, with others.
 We are each other's teachers.
 Let us, therefore, make certain
 the unconditional loving messages
 we share always help others,
 rather than harm them, leaving
 our children a world of hope,
 rather than despair.

The Journey

We each follow a different path
    on our journey through life.
    Though there are an endless
    number of turns in the road,
    detouring us each in an infinite
    number of directions, the
    destination is the same;
    uniting with our spirit within.
    Sharing its inherent wisdom and
    unconditional love selflessly with
    others to help each reunite with
    their spirit as well, will complete
    our life's journey, and bring genuine
    meaning to our lives as well.

Why Are We Alive?

Are we alive just to make money,
    have a family, prestigious job,
    buy nice things, and do everything
    we were told would make us
    happy and live a meaningful life?
    In reality, everything we were
    told that would allow us to be
    happy, find love and meaning
    in our life is an illusion,
    propagated by our learned beliefs.
    These things may not be
    found in a self-centered world.
    They must first be discovered
    within, then selflessly shared to
    help others find happiness, love,
    and meaning in their life as well.

God

The belief in god influences
many people throughout the
world; therefore, the awareness
of god must not be ignored.
Whether you call god spirit,
soul, essence, or by any other
name, this ethereal being has been
the subject of much discussion
and division throughout time.
Though god should unite us,
often our differing beliefs
in god divide us instead.
Every life, regardless of our
religion, beliefs, or any other
differences, is equally important.
No one life or belief, is or ever
has been, better or more
important than another's.
There is a small piece of god
present within every life,
inextricably connecting
each of us to the other.
It is only when we realize
this and selflessly share this
part of us with each other
that the spiritual evolution of
our planet may finally begin.

Each Life is Extraordinary

We are all one in a crowd
    of many, hidden from
    view by the multitude.
    Yet each life is extraordinary,
    unique, having the ability to
    change the world, not by
    their accomplishments or
    prestige, but by selflessly
    sharing their inherent wisdom
    and unconditional love, their
    spirit, with others, changing
    their lives forever by doing so.

To the Children of the World

As you are growing up, you
will notice life can appear
to be very challenging.
The world is not always a
very nice place to live in.
You will see many things that
make you wonder why bad
things happen to so many.
You will see people who do
not have enough food to eat
or a place to live, and others,
who do not like someone
because they are different.
Regardless of what color
your skin is, the country you
live in, your beliefs, or any
other differences there are
between us, it is important
you do not believe anyone
is better or more important
than anyone else.
Every life is equally important,
regardless of any differences
there are between us.
Living a good life has nothing
to do with the job you have,
the amount of money you make,
if you are famous, or anything
else you may hear about
when you are growing up.
Rather, the only important thing
is that you are a good person.
Be someone who truly cares

about others feelings, helping
them whenever you can, treating
everyone with kindness and
love, even if they do not
treat you that way.
You will find there are many
in the world who are unhappy,
afraid, and worry only about themselves.
Please, do not be like them.
You can change the world if you
simply listen to the quiet voice
in your heart and share the loving
messages you hear with others.
Embrace life with awe.
Be kind to everyone.
Share the goodness in your
heart with those who are
different or struggling.
And, most importantly, treat
others like you wish to be treated.
If you do this, you will be happy.
Choose not to live in a world
where everyone is afraid,
worrying only about themselves.
Instead, be compassionate loving,
respectful, humble, and
optimistic about life.
Be courageous.
Care about others feelings.
Be friendly and help them if
they are different or in need.
If you do this, you may find your
life will be happy and meaningful.
The path you choose through life
will decide the future of the world.

The older generations have not
done a very good job taking care
of our planet or each other.
It is up to you, therefore, our
children, to make the changes
that must be made, by always
choosing the loving path in life.

We Are All Equal, Important, and Connected

It does not matter what job
 you have, how much money
 you make, the color of your
 skin, your ethnicity, religious
 preference, or any other
 comparison we may make.
 We are all equal, important,
 and connected.
 Only when everyone succeeds
 in life, regardless of our
 differences, will our
 lives truly have meaning.

How Do You Know When You Are Awake?

Instead of seeing only
    the worse in people,
    you will now begin to
    see the good in others.
    Instead of darkness,
    you will see light.
    Instead of helplessness,
    you will now want to
    selflessly help others.
    Instead of accepting living
    in a world of fear, you will
    want to help change the
    world, allowing others to
    live in a world of love,
    compassion, and hope instead.

Our Primary Guide

Once we accept the spirit,
  present to guide our life
  with its inherent wisdom
  and unconditional love,
  rather than the ego, our
  self-centered learned beliefs,
  as our primary guide through
  life, we may begin a quest to
  discover the genuine purpose
  of our life's journey.

The Dream

When we are born,
    the dream begins.
    For most, it will continue
    unabated until the
    moment of their death.
    Everything we see, learn
    about, and accept is true
    becomes a repetitive dream
    we have every day.
    We remain asleep when we
    accept everything we learned
    about living in a self-
    centered world is true,
    believing there is little we
    may do to change the world.
    There are those who may begin
    to awaken from their slumber,
    sensing the first messages
    from their spirit within.
    With this partial arousal,
    they start to question if what
    they have been dreaming
    about was true.
    We finally may wake up from
    our dream, when we truly
    understand little we had
    dreamed about was real.
    It was all a myth, an illusion,
    created by the ego, our learned
    beliefs, to control our lives,
    and convince us of our

importance in the world.

To Know Another

When you see another do you
    only look at their appearance?
    When you talk with another do
    you only hear their spoken words?
    To genuinely know another look
    deeper, beyond the superficial
    layers, the façade, we project,
    by seeing and hearing our
    essence within, embracing
    who we truly are, rather
    than just the illusion we
    project to the world.

Every Life is Equally Valuable

No one, regardless of wealth,
    prestige, or any other perceived
    differences, is better or more
    important than another.
    Though some may believe
    they are due to the color of
    their skin, sex, religion, or any
    of the many other distinctions
    between us, they never have been.
    This belief is the underlying cause
    of war, prejudice, inequity, and all
    of humanity's self-inflicted
    challenges and harmful emotions
    existing throughout the ages.
    To change the future and leave
    a better world for our children,
    we must recognize every life's
    equal value, treating each
    as we ourselves hope
    others will treat us.

Do Not Fear Death

It is not important when
    you die; it is how you live
    that will define your life.
    Wealth, material possessions,
    living to old age, or anything
    else we learn and believe is
    important to have led a good
    life, will not impede death.
    As death approaches and many
    review their life, often, they
    may realize none of the things
    they thought would define
    their life mattered; that their
    life, though it may have
    been successful, was not
    meaningful or important.
    A poor homeless child, dying
    at a very young age, embracing
    the innate wisdom and unconditional
    loving messages of their spirit
    within before their early demise,
    may have led a more profound
    life then one much older and
    more successful than they were.
    It is how we live our life,
    selflessly sharing the wisdom
    and messages of eternal love
    to help others, that will
    ultimately define our life
    when death inevitably approaches.

What Do You See?

When you look at the
    world what do you see?
    Do you see light or
    darkness; love or hate?
    Allowing life to dictate
    your future, accepting all
    the false things you learned
    were true, you will only
    see darkness and hate.
    Allowing your loving spirit,
    however, your higher-self,
    to direct your path through
    life instead, light and love will
    be seen in every person and
    challenge you encounter in life.

A Deep Need

One day, a gnawing deep
    sensation may be felt,
    wondering if there is a reason,
    a purpose for our existence.
    We begin to consider if there
    may be more to life than just
    making money, having a family,
    buying material possessions,
    enjoying ourselves.
    Though we may have all
    these things, it does not
    satisfy the unsatiable intense
    need we feel within to find
    out if there may be more.
    Most go through life asleep,
    unaware there is more to life
    than doing all the things we
    learned will allow us
    to live a successful life.
    It is only when we begin to
    embrace our spirit within as
    the primary guide through life,
    we may start to wake from our
    slumber and begin to satisfy this
    inherent urge to discover if
    there may be a different, more
    profound reason, we are alive.

How Many Must Die?

How many more innocents
    must die before we wake
    from our slumber?
    How many more families
    must be destroyed?
    The world, and all life
    on it, is on a precipice,
    overlooking a deep abyss.
    If humanity continues on
    the destructive path they
    are on, climate change,
    disease, nuclear war, or
    some other man-made
    catastrophe will end the
    suffering of all life, leaving
    only an uninhabitable
    empty shell where a once
    vibrant planet had existed.
    To step back from the
    abyss, we must end these
    senseless deaths, reject
    hate and fear, replacing it
    instead with unconditional
    love and courage.

We Are Each Part of a Whole

We are one of many.
　　Every life is unique, special,
　　yet we share a common purpose.
　　Though we may appear different,
　　have distinct personalities and
　　beliefs, we are inextricably
　　linked by a universal entity
　　present within every life.
　　Look past what you see,
　　judge, hear, believe to
　　the spirit within another.
　　It is there you will finally
　　understand we are all
　　connected, we are one,
　　part of a universal collective,
　　alive to selflessly help each
　　other by sharing our spirit's
　　inherent wisdom and
　　unconditional love, as we
　　each journey through life together.

Look Deeper

When you talk, see, hear
    another, gaze beyond the
    superficial 'I' they present,
    to their authentic-self, their
    spirit, present within each.
    See the beauty they
    radiate from within.
    Sense the words of
    unconditional love
    emanating from their heart.
    Everything else is an illusion,
    a myth learned after we were
    born, accepted as real,
    dictated by others as the truth.
    It never was.

What Defines Us?

Who are we?
    Are we our race, sex, religion,
    job, or anything else we
    were told defines us?
    Are we our essence, soul,
    spirit, a piece of god present
    within every life to give our
    lives meaning by guiding us
    with its innate wisdom and
    unconditional love so
    we may help others?
    We are both.
    We each must decide
    though, which to primarily
    follow through life.
    One will lead to the
    continuation of the status
    quo and the many harmful
    challenges this path encourages.
    The other to discovering
    genuine meaning in our life and
    to humanity's spiritual evolution.
    Let us choose wisely for
    the future of our planet and all
    life on it which rely on its grace.

The Fork in the Road

There are but two paths we
    may choose through life.
    Though we each must travel
    our own individual journey,
    we have a choice which
    path we will take.
    The path of fear, which
    represents accepting the
    self-centered views of the
    world, or the path of
    unconditional love, present
    within every life, representing
    the unlimited possibilities
    living in a caring, loving
    world allows.
    One path leads to endless struggle,
    stress, and the continuation
    of the status quo.
    The other to a genuine
    understanding about
    our life's purpose.
    To find the path you desire,
    when you come to the fork
    in the road, choose the
    steeper more difficult path,
    listening to the quiet messages
    you sense within, rather than
    the loud chaotic ones you
    were taught to believe were true.

~ ~

Don't miss out!

Visit the website below and you can sign up to receive emails whenever Ken Luball publishes a new book. There's no charge and no obligation.

https://books2read.com/r/B-A-VKSR-UXNVB

BOOKS 2 READ

Connecting independent readers to independent writers.

Did you love *The Spirit Guide: Journey Through Life*? Then you should read *Tranquility: A Village of Hope*[2] by Ken Luball!

Tranquility: A Village of Hope is book 3 in *The Awakening Tetralogy*.

Raised by the Enlightened. Guided by Wisdom. Called to Share.

Nestled deep in the Canadian Rocky Mountains lies Tranquility, a hidden village where peace, wisdom, and spiritual awakening are part of everyday life. In this third installment of *The Awakening Tetralogy*, young Elke is born into a community unlike any other—surrounded by enlightened souls from Tranquility and a neighboring First Nations village.

As she journeys through life, Elke shares the powerful spiritual lessons passed on to her—lessons about love, ego, truth, and inner peace. Through simple storytelling and profound insight, *Tranquility: A Village of Hope* gently invites readers to reflect, awaken, and reconnect with their true self.

---

2. https://books2read.com/u/bpw2eW

3. https://books2read.com/u/bpw2eW

Whether you're beginning your spiritual path or deepening your awakening, this heart-centered novel offers hope, healing, and a return to stillness.

Read more at kenluball.com.

About the Author

My name is Ken Luball ~ Spiritual ~ Seeker ~ Author
****

Author of:

'*Our Search for Meaning*' – a series of three books of thoughtful easily understandable spiritual reflections about awakening, enlightenment, spirituality, & the meaning of life.
****

'*Spiritual Reflections*' – Two books of spiritual reflections using metaphor, imagery, and spiritual insight to explore themes of awakening, enlightenment, and the human pursuit of meaning.
****

<u>'*The Awakening Tetralogy*': A series of four spiritual novels</u>
The first three stories in The Awakening Tetralogy are written in the first person, following the spiritual journey through life of a child, as they learn the lessons needed during their life to awaken and become enlightened.

Today I Am Going to Die: Choices in Life
The Spirit Guide: Journey Through Life
Tranquility: A Village of Hope
The Illusion of Happiness: Choosing Love Over Fear
****

Links for each of these 9 books on website.
****

Ever since I was a young child, I knew my purpose in life; it was for me to awaken, find enlightenment, and share my experience and knowledge with others. To reach those lofty aspirations though, I first had to navigate through quite a few unexpected detours in my life.

It took me almost an entire lifetime to truly understand what this meant. It is my hope you will read my books, and in doing so, begin a new adventure; one where you will awaken and further your journey toward enlightenment with your spirit within.

Read more at kenluball.com.